AN ANGRY ACCUSATION

They dragged Torridon straight in before old John Brett, and the latter regarded him with bent brows.

"Paul Torridon," said he, "I've been keeping you in my house for twelve years or more. I've kept you in food and clothes and I've given you easy work. Your own father wouldn't've treated you half as good. How've you paid me back?"

Torridon looked earnestly back into the face of the clansman. It was not contorted with anger. It was simply hard and cold. He glanced rapidly at the others. Their passion was less under control than that of their leader. They stared at him with hungry malice . . .

"Uncle John," said Torridon earnestly, "will you tell me what I have to gain by an attack on the house of Harry Brett?"

"What has any Torridon to gain?" asked John Brett. "What have the snakes in the field to gain by sneaking up and biting a man that's sleeping?"

Torridon was silenced . . . Charles Brett stepped in from the side and struck him heavily in the face. The blow knocked him with a crash against the wall. He staggered back onto the floor, his head spinning. The hard knuckles of Charlie had split the skin over his cheek bone and a trickle of blood ran down rapidly . . .

Books by Max Brand
From The Berkley Publishing Group

THE BIG TRAIL
BORDER GUNS
CHEYENNE GOLD
COWARD OF THE CLAN
DAN BARRY'S DAUGHTER
DEVIL HORSE
DRIFTER'S VENGEANCE
THE FASTEST DRAW
FLAMING IRONS
FRONTIER FEUD
THE GALLOPING BRONCOS
THE GAMBLER
THE GENTLE GUNMAN
GOLDEN LIGHTNING
GUNMAN'S GOLD
THE GUNS OF DORKING HOLLOW
THE INVISIBLE OUTLAW
THE LONG CHASE
LOST WOLF
LUCKY LARRIBEE
MIGHTY LOBO
MONTANA RIDES
MYSTERY RANCH
THE NIGHTHAWK TRAIL
ONE MAN POSSE
OUTLAW BREED
OUTLAW'S CODE
THE REVENGE OF BROKEN ARROW
RIDERS OF THE SILENCES
RUSTLERS OF BEACON CREEK
SILVERTIP
SILVERTIP'S CHASE
SPEEDY
THE STRANGER
TAMER OF THE WILD
TENDERFOOT
TORTURE TRAIL
TRAILIN'
TRAIL PARTNERS
TWENTY NOTCHES
WAR PARTY
THE WHITE WOLF

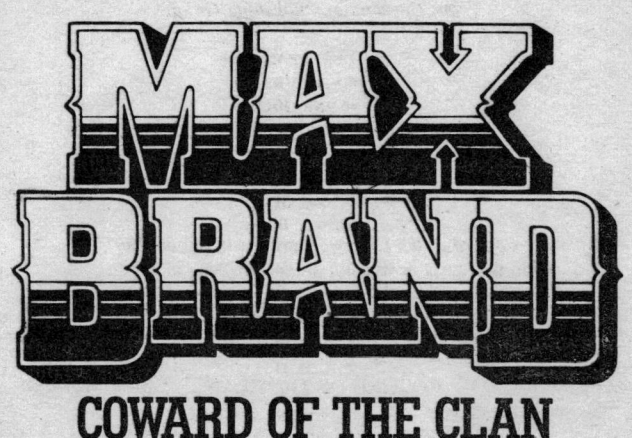

COWARD OF THE CLAN

BOOKS BY MAIL SERVICE
120 S. COLLEGE
TAHLEQUAH, OK 74464

BERKLEY BOOKS, NEW YORK

Coward of the Clan was previously published
in two parts in *Western Story Magazine* in 1928
under the titles *Coward of the Clan* and
The Man from the Sky, written under the
pseudonym of Peter Henry Morland.

COWARD OF THE CLAN

A Berkley Book / published by arrangement with
G. P. Putnam's Sons

PRINTING HISTORY
Berkley edition/January 1991
Published simultaneously in hardcover
by G. P. Putnam's Sons.

All rights reserved.
Copyright © 1991 by Santa Barbara Bank and Trust.
This book may not be reproduced in whole or in part, by
mimeograph or any other means, without permission.
For information address: G. P. Putnam's Sons,
200 Madison Avenue, New York, New York 10016.

ISBN: 0-425-12529-7

A BERKLEY BOOK® TM 757,375
Berkley Books are published by The Berkley Publishing Group,
200 Madison Avenue, New York, New York 10016.
The name "BERKLEY" and the "B" logo
are trademarks belonging to Berkley Publishing Corporation.

PRINTED IN THE UNITED STATES OF AMERICA

10 9 8 7 6 5 4 3 2 1

PART ONE
★
Coward of the Clan

CHAPTER I

★

What's in a Name?

The first thing that Paul Torridon remembered was being led by the hand to a tall man with long hair and a short gray beard, a beard that was chopped off brutally, for convenience rather than for appearance. Seen from the back with his curls flowing down over his shoulders, John Brett looked the portrait of some chivalrous cavalier. Seen from the front with that blunt stub of a beard, he seemed partly grotesque, partly savage. To heighten the contrast, his beard had turned white while his hair still remained a glossy, youthful black.

Of what had gone before, Paul Torridon had no idea, but something about the face of this giant pierced his mind and remained in his thoughts forever.

"Is this one of them? Is this one of them?" shouted John Brett. "Why did you bring this thing home to me?"

"Shall I take him back and turn him loose in the woods?" asked the man who held the hand of Paul. "That'll answer the same purpose."

"You fool!" cried Brett. "You blathering, hopeless fool. You've brought him inside my house, haven't you? Turn him over to the women and never let me see his face."

How the women received him, Paul Torridon forgot, except for one flash of recollection which had to do with an old crone who shook her finger at his head and groaned: "He'll bring harm to us all!"

Then the mists closed again around the mind of Paul Torridon.

He should have remembered much more, for he was well over seven years of age and, of course, far advanced into the period of full memory, but something had shocked the past into total oblivion, or else there was a sense of mere shadows moving among shadows, in the beginning.

His recollection of the past was cut like a thread, and at the same time his knowledge of the present washed away in waves, to-day carrying off in its withdrawal yesterday, and all the days before; so that for some time to come his only surviving sense of that period was that he had been surrounded by cloth, a world of homespun in drab colors, the enormous skirts of the women, and the bulky coats of the men.

He could see, later, that this was the time during which he was left exclusively to the hands of the women, and so he came by degrees out into the open light of full memory, full understanding.

He used to help the women at the milking of the cows. Once as he was bringing in a three-gallon pail half filled, the giant, John Brett, loomed suddenly before him.

"What's your name?" asked John Brett.

"Paul Torridon."

The face of John Brett grew black.

"As quick as the bell answers the bell hammer," said he.

He turned away, but poor little Torridon was so frightened that the milk pail fell to the ground and spilled a white tide across the mud. He knew that he would be beaten, but a whip could not fill his mind with terror as did the mere echo of the voice of John Brett.

He came upon one great and important truth—that there was something wrong with the name Torridon; and there was something right in the name Brett. Every one around the place was a Brett. The house of John Brett, in fact, was hardly a house so much as it was a village gathered hodgepodge under one roof. There was a blacksmith, a carpenter, a shoemaker, for instance. There was a storekeeper, even. And all these people, and those who plowed in the fields and rode off hunting through the mountains, bore the name of Brett. To the dawning intelligence of

Paul Torridon it appeared that the world was filled with the name of Brett; for on holidays and Sundays, sometimes, strangers rode up. They were all big men on big horses, like those who lived under the roof of John Brett. And these visitors, too, carried the name of Brett.

Paul began to feel that his name was a freak, just as he himself was a freak compared to the sons of the house—he was so slenderly made, so delicate, and they were so big and brawny. Once Charles Brett, who was a little younger than Paul, took both the boy's hands in one of his and crushed them with his grip. Paul wrenched and pulled. At last he cried out with the pain and began to weep. Charles Brett looked at him, agape, and dropped the tortured hand.

"You're just like a girl, ain't you?" remarked Charlie.

There were other Torridons. But they were far away. All by that name on the western side of the mountains had been wiped out in that night of blood and fire which had blotted the mind of Paul. The only Torridons who remained in all the world lived on the eastern side of the mountains. There let them remain, unless the Bretts should decide to strike even at that distance and, riding through the passes, storm down on the enemy and smash them.

Charlie Brett used to talk about that. And he would end: "Then there'll be no Torridon left but you!" With that he would laugh triumphantly, mockingly.

Later Paul learned that in the distant past the Bretts and the Torridons had been so matched in strength that each side occasionally won a battle.

John Brett kept Paul for two years without further important remark. Then he met little Paul in a hall of the house and seemed startled at seeing him.

"Are you still around? Are you still around?" he exclaimed gloomily. "You're growin' up, too."

He took Torridon by the shoulder and pushed him toward the light. There he examined his face thoughtfully.

"You're growin' up," he repeated. "In a couple of years there'll be enough poison in you to kill a man—and a Brett!"

"I never would kill a man," said Paul.

"You're a Torridon, ain't you?" asked John Brett.

Paul began to cry.

"Why are you whimpering?" asked John Brett curiously. "Have I hurt you?"

"I don't know," said Paul. "I can't help crying. You—you make me tremble inside!"

John Brett went away.

Afterward Torridon was told that he was to be taken over the mountains to his kin, but two days after this he was ill with scarlet fever.

The summer went before he was strong enough to walk. In the spring of his tenth year a cow broke his leg with a kick. And another summer passed during which he was incapable of traveling. Bad luck dogged him. When he was twelve, pneumonia reduced him to a mere trembling wisp of a body. At thirteen he had not recovered. He was so weak that even Aunt Ellen Brett, that cruel and keen old woman who managed the household, forbade him to be given outdoor work. He was employed in the kitchen to scrub pans and light fires and carry in wood from the shed; in the long evenings he was set to work helping the women spin.

Now in the fourteenth year of his life two great events happened. One affected the entire clan. One had to do with Paul Torridon alone.

The first thing was the foaling of the black colt, and the reason it was of such importance was that John Brett had been hoping for twenty years to produce a colt of that color. For in the old days he had owned a great black stallion, Nineveh, still famous through all the country—a sort of legendary flyer. People said of a horse that it was "as fast as Nineveh," "as strong as Nineveh," just as they might say that a man was as strong as Hercules. All the horses which the Bretts rode were descended directly from that famous stallion, but there was never his like again and, strange to say, in all his get there appeared the pure black strain only twice, and these were mares and of little note.

Now, however, after twenty years of waiting, a black colt was foaled. The whole clan swept from the house—man, woman, child—and stood in the pasture in a large open circle.

The mother was an undistinguished creature, with a backbone thrusting up like a mountain ridge and a vast prominence of hips. Ewe-necked, lump-headed, she was like an ugly spot in the fine race which had descended from Nineveh. But her foal was another matter.

He was black as coal. There was not a hair of white on any of his legs. There was not a hair of white about his muzzle, or on his forehead, nor in his tail. He was one entire jet carving.

He looked to Paul Torridon like any other foal, except that he appeared a good bit on the clumsy, heavy side; but John Brett's face was working with delight. There was nothing about the colt that did not please him. He pointed out the slope of the shoulders, the depth at the heart, the huge bone.

"I gotta have a name for him," said John Brett.

"Nineveh Second," suggested Charles.

"He ain't a second Nineveh. He's gunna be better than that!" cried John Brett in great excitement.

No one dared to question the head of the clan, but at this speech heads were turned and covert smiles exchanged.

"What's a name like Nineveh?" cried John Brett. "Nineveh was a town, wasn't it?"

"It was a town in the Bible," answered another.

"Who knows something about it?" asked John Brett.

He swept the circle with a stern glance. "Where's the book-learning in this family? Where's the women that had ought to know about Bibles and books and things? Do the men have to stay home and waste their time?"

The women looked gloomily upon one another. They might have pointed out that if the men were busy with hunting and farming, the women were still busier with mending, sewing, spinning, weaving, milking, cooking, housecleaning; but no one, not even Aunt Ellen, dared to lift a voice when the master of the clan was in temper.

"Nobody!" cried John Brett, his gray beard quivering with wrath. "Nobody! Nobody knows nothing!"

A voice had been rising in Paul Torridon. It had been a great, bold voice when it started at his heart. It was the faintest of squeaking whispers when it came to his lips.

"I do," said he.

He was not heard, except by Aunt Ellen, who was near him. She caught him by the shoulder and shook him violently.

"You do?" she asked. "D'you know something about it? Hey, John Brett, here's one that can talk about it!"

She thrust the boy out from the circle. For the first time in his life all eyes were upon him and not in scorn. Instead there was wonder, interest, hushed attention. Even John Brett was stirred.

"You know sump'n about Nineveh?" he asked, making his voice gentler than usual.

"Yes," said Paul, but the words made no sound upon his lips.

"Speak out, Paul," said the big man, still more quietly.

"I—I'll try," said Paul, his eyes almost straining from his head.

"Go on, then. Was Nineveh a town?"

"It was," said Paul.

"What kind of a town?"

"A great city," said Paul.

"Like Louisville?"

"It was much larger."

"Hey? Like Philadelphia, then?"

"It was larger," said Paul.

"Like New York?"

"Yes," said Paul.

John Brett was filled with admiration.

"Now, that's a dog-gone queer thing," he remarked. "There's a town as big as New York that's disappeared so complete that if it didn't have its name tucked away into the Bible, we'd never 've had a horse named after it. Now, Paul, I want a name that's got something to do with this here city. Gimme one, can you?"

The mind of Paul Torridon went round and round.

"Say something, you little putty-faced fool!" said Aunt Ellen in a savage whisper.

John Brett raised his brows and turned his frown upon her. She shrank back in silence.

"It was in Assyria," said Paul.

"Ah-ha!" cried John Brett. "That's pretty good. It was in Assyria. How would Assyria do for a name for that colt?"

"It ain't got sound enough to it," suggested some one.

"No. It ain't got enough sound to it," agreed John Brett. "Now that Assyria, it would have a king, wouldn't it, Paul?"

"Yes, sir," answered Paul, who was recovering some of his self-control.

The entire circle was waiting breathless upon him and his answers.

"It *would* have a king, he says," proceeded John Brett in the same half-anxious, half-soothing tone. "Now, Paul, that there colt is gunna be a king. He's gunna be a big, black king among hosses. Look at him. Don't be afraid. He's just makin' up to you, Paul!"

The black foal approached the boy with sharply pricked ears and began to nibble at his sleeve.

Paul dared not stir.

"Now, Paul," went on John Brett, "might you be able to tell me something like the name of a king of Assyria?"

"Yes," said Paul. "They had some very long names."

"You even know their names?" said Brett curiously.

And a stir of wonder ran rapidly around the circle.

"Some of them," said Paul. "There was Sennacherib, for instance, and—"

"Sennacherib! That's a longish name, and hard to get a tongue around. Now, Paul, could you think of some of the other names?"

"Yes," said the boy, "there was Merodach-baladam, and Shalmaneser, and Tiglath Pileser and—"

"Hold on, will you?" gasped John Brett. "Them names—I never heard nothing like them! But who was the biggest and the greatest king that they had, if you know, Paul?"

"Ashur-bani-pal was the greatest king," said Paul.

"Ashur-bani-pal," repeated John Brett slowly. "We don't seem to get along very well, do we?"

The mare, anxious about her foal, came up behind the boy and sniffed at his neck; her breath sent a shudder through all his body.

"Steady!" said John Brett. "Steady, my boy! She ain't gunna hurt you a mite. Only—I don't see how names could be that long, even in a Bible country like Assyria."

"The names really have several words in them," said Paul, wanting to run from the mare but not daring to move.

"Like what?"

"Ashur-bani-pal means 'Ashur creates a son.'"

"And who was Ashur?"

"Ashur was the chief god. He was the war god."

"And here's the chief hoss, and a war hoss," said John Brett, "and there's the name for him. Ashur is it! And you, Paul, how'd you come to know all this rigmarole about Assyria, and what not?"

CHAPTER II

★

Cold Water

The answers which young Torridon had made to the questions of John Brett had been attended by the rest of the clan with a most hushed interest, but to no answer did they give stricter heed than to the present one, when Paul said simply: "I've been sick a great deal, you know. And I had nothing to do but lie in bed and read."

"Well," said John Brett, "then I think I'll put some of the other children to bed for a while!"

This brought a laugh, and in the laughter Paul was able to slip away. But he was vastly pleased. Never before had he been looked on with respect by the others. Certainly he never had been such a center of attention.

This was not the end of the incident; it was the beginning of a new phase in the life of Paul. From that moment he was some one in the community of the Bretts. Even old Aunt Ellen, regarding him with her overbright eyes, said afterward: "He's got a brain behind those eyes of his!"

He repeated that saying over and over again to himself for days and days afterward. He had a brain. The others had their great, strong bodies, their great, strong hands; he had a brain! The first spark of pride fell on his soul, and the fire was beginning to burn.

It burned exceedingly small, however, at first. There was need of much tinder of the most delicate sort to feed the flame, and only gradually he came to realize that his position in the household was altered. He had to do the same things as before. But there was a touch of respect on all hands. The Bretts valued in man little other than force of hand and courage of heart, but Paul Torridon they began to accept as an oddity with a sort of strength as great as his weakness.

In the early autumn John Brett summoned the boy one evening and told him to bring in all the books which he had read.

They made several loads. He heaped them on the table. Books were an accident in the Brett household, but there was an arithmetic, and an algebra of vast antiquity, a good old-fashioned grammar, a history of the ancient world, a thick tome from which the cover was entirely missing and the title page gone as well. This, together with a Bible and a "Pilgrim's Progress," constituted the backbone of the reading of young Paul. The rest consisted of a miscellaneous assortment, from almanacs to novels. Not one of those books had been bought intentionally by the Bretts, but all had been taken in gathering in the effects of a bankrupt neighbor who could pay his debts in no way except through his goods. They had lain in an attic unnoticed for years, while the rats ate through many of them. There Paul Torridon had found them, and through the long months and months of his illnesses, he had worked over them with the patience of despair. Even the problems in the arithmetic and the algebra were a delight, and when the last of them was solved he had fallen into a profound gloom.

Now he stood by the table and saw John Brett, with thick and unaccustomed fingers, turning the frail leaves of the books. Delicately and carefully he handled them, as though in fear lest they rend like spider's silk under his touch.

He remarked finally: "There's thirty-five books here!"

"Yes," said Paul.

"You've read them all?"

"Yes. Several times over."

The big man lifted his brows. He rested his chin on the hard palm of his hand and stared.

"Several times? You mean that?"

"This one a great many times," said the boy, and touched the ponderous ancient history.

Coward of the Clan ☆ 13

"How come that?"

"After pneumonia, you remember it was weeks and weeks before I could leave my bed, and I had only this book in the room."

"And you read that?"

"Four times through, carefully."

"Didn't you get tired of it?"

"No, because I never was able to remember everything in it."

"Why didn't you send for some of the other books?"

"I did ask for them. Nobody wanted to go."

The glance of Brett sharpened again. Then he looked suddenly aside. That small remark evidently had meant something to him. He sent the boy off to bed, but a week later, when the first frost began, he conversed with Paul again.

"Your fifteen, Paul?"

"Yes, sir."

"You've been here eight years?"

"Yes, sir."

"Are you willin' to work?"

"I'm willing to do what I can."

"Education is pretty good," observed John Brett. "I'm gunna make a school, with you for the teacher, and every man and boy up to twenty in the whole tribe is gunna come and study under you, and all the girls up to fifteen. Can you teach 'em?"

Paul Torridon was aghast, but he dared not refuse.

He lay awake that night, staring at the darkness. He tried to think of himself imposing tasks upon Charles Brett, for instance. The thought was unthinkable!

However, the plan went forward. Whatever John Brett determined upon, he put through with suddenness and with effect. The three clans of the Bretts lived at equal distances from one another. They were like the three points of a triangle. Almost in the center was a crossroads. There John Brett called a meeting of the heads of the families, and there he struck his heel into the ground and declared that the schoolhouse must be posted.

The others agreed. They dared not dispute with him, any more than soldiers would have dared to dispute with a general. They lived in a sea of dangers, and they knew the value of the leadership of this rough, rude man. The schoolhouse was built in two weeks. A stove was installed in the center of it. Paul Torridon was told to meet his first class.

Pale from a sleepless night, he walked out over the frosty, white road, stumbling in the ruts uncertainly. The boots which the Brett shoemaker turned out were only roughly shaped to the foot. And these which Torridon wore were castoffs of Charlie Brett. His feet slipped about in them awkwardly. And three shanks as large as his could have fitted into the tops. His coat, too, was a discard. Much scrubbing with soap had faded and worn the tough homespun but had not dimmed the splendor of the grease spots with which it was checkered. It was rubbed through at either elbow, and was so big that he wrapped it around him and pinned one edge of it above his right hip. His hat was a battered, green-faded thing which lay without shape on his head, the brim falling down over his eyes.

There was so little strength in Torridon that he was wearied without being warmed by the walk. Neither can the weak enjoy the beauty of a winter scene, and he looked about him in despair at the naked trees, their limbs outlined with broken pipings of white frost. He saw no living thing except, on a bare bough, a row of little birds, with their feathers all ruffed out and their heads drawn in until they seemed little, round, headless balls.

He yearned with all his heart to be back in the kitchen at the house of John Brett, or even amid the sour smells of the creamery. Everything that was familiar was cheering to him. Everything that was strange was a load upon his mind.

When he came in sight of the schoolhouse, he halted. His legs were powerless to carry him forward. It was not until the chill thrust through his very vitals that he spurred forward and with slow steps approached the door.

He opened it with a desperate thrust of his hand and stepped quickly inside. His greeting was the tumbling of a bucket of water which had been propped above the door by a practical jester. He was drenched to the skin and stood shivering in a wild outburst of laughter.

In that roar of mirth were the voices of twenty-year-old youths, brutalized by heavy labor and exposure all the days of their lives. There was the shouting of girls almost as brown and strong as their brothers, and the shrill piping of children.

In the midst of that dreadful mockery, Paul Torridon shuddered and turned blue with the cold of the water. He went to the stove, wrung the water from his coat, and then spread his hands close to the heated iron.

He looked around him, his head jerking with nervousness. Seventeen grinning faces looked back at him, expectant, scornful, contemptuous. Only one looked neither at him nor at her companions, but down at her folded hands. That was Nancy Brett.

CHAPTER III

★

David And Goliath

He could not make himself warm.

He could only thaw the outer layers of the cold, as it were. Then he went to his desk. It was raised on a little platform at the end of the room. It consisted of a table with two drawers on either side. A subdued murmuring was sweeping from one side of the room to the other; the grinning faces watched him, brightly, as mischievous dogs watch a cat they are about to pounce on. Nancy Brett had raised her head and watched him, also, but gravely, with a veil over her eyes, so to speak.

He was more conscious of her quiet scorn than of all the unmasked grins of the rest.

"We'd better start," said Paul hoarsely, "with writing down our names. You all have slates and slate pencils. Please write down your names!"

He sat down and waited. There was only one who stirred to obey, and that was Nancy Brett.

For five minutes he waited. Then he rose from his chair. His face was icy cold, and he knew that it must be deadly white. Directly opposite his desk was big Jack Brett, burly six-footer, twenty years old, dark as an Indian, and as savage. He sat with arms folded, waiting, sneering.

Paul started for him, met that sneer, and hesitated.

He looked wildly about him. In the farther corner he saw Charles Brett drop his head and turn crimson, and he knew that Charlie was blushing with hot shame to think that one who had lived under the same roof with him should be such a helpless coward. But most of all, Paul saw Nancy, whose eyes were averted toward the window and whose face was pale also.

And then a sudden thought came to him with a blessed relief. After all, he could not do more than die, and death itself would be the open door through which he would escape from this flamboyant mockery, this scorn, this contemptuous world in which all his days were so wretched.

He went straight up to big Jack.

"Can you write?" he asked.

"Young feller," said Jack, bending dark brows, "are you sassin' me, maybe?"

The room hushed to delicious expectancy.

"If you can write," said Paul, "why haven't you put down your name?"

The big fellow grinned. He searched inward for insulting phrases, but all he could find to say was: "Maybe I'm gunna write it and maybe I ain't. Maybe I ain't ready to write it. And you—what you gunna do about it? Do I get a licking?"

He leered at Paul out of the greatness of his strength. Death, certainly, was coming upon the teacher. So, at least, he felt. Those mighty hands could break him like a reed; those balled fists, like ragged lumps of iron, could smash straight through his body.

And across the mind of Paul came an echo from an old romance which he had read in one of his times of illness. In that book, ringed with enemies, the hero had bidden the most formidable of them all to come from the house with him and settle their differences in solitude.

Now he quoted from it, word for word: "Will you leave the room with me, sir?"

That "sir" might have caused more comment, but the excitement was so tense that it was passed over.

"And why'n earth should I leave the room with you?" asked big Jack.

Almost in those words the brute of the novel had spoken, and the hero had answered as Paul answered now: "There are women here. Do you wish them to see blood?"

Big Jack lurched to his feet. He was half of a mind to knock down the little school-teacher then and there, but Paul already was moving uncertainly toward the door. He found it through a mist, and stepped out into the cold, clear morning.

Jack strode behind him. Like a giant he seemed as he stood with feet braced at the bottom of the steps.

"Now what do you want?" he asked savagely.

"I want you," said the young teacher, "to go home to your father and tell him that you have refused to do what I asked you to do. Or else go back into the school and begin to work."

There was a gasp from the massed faces at the door. The handsome face of Jack grew scarlet with anger.

"And if I don't do either, then what?"

"Then," said Paul, "I'll have to try to make you."

"Well," snarled Jack, "I ain't gunna do neither. And you try to make me, kid. I ask you that!"

"Very well," said Paul. He looked at those balled fists with a sigh. The stronger and harder they were, the better. Death would be utterly painless. "Very well," said Paul, and stepping a little closer, he flicked big Jack lightly across the face with his open hand.

The answer was all that Paul could have prayed for. It was totally painless. It seemed that a heavy blow fell on the base of his brain, and he dropped into a thousand leagues of darkness.

When he recovered, the sun was spinning across the face of the sky in vast circles. The schoolhouse fairly dissolved in the speed with which it whirled. The trees near by blurred together.

"He's alive!" cried a deep, heavy voice.

"Lift him up and carry him in from this frosty ground," said the voice of a girl.

Paul closed his eyes again, and the darkness shot over his brain once more in a long, slow wave, beginning at his feet.

He wakened near the heat of the stove. A cold cloth was across his forehead. He raised his hand to a bulging, painful lump on the side of his jaw. That was where the blow had fallen. How strange that it had not broken the bone, snapped his neck, smashed all before it!

He could not see clearly, but when that same heavy man's voice spoke again, he recognized the tones of big Jack.

"How's the back of your head, Paul? Will you feel it there—where it whacked the ground?"

Paul obediently fumbled at the spot. It was a little sore, but there seemed nothing wrong.

"It ain't fractured?" gasped Jack.

"No. I'm all right. I—"

"Lie still, will you? Lie still and—Nancy, what'd we better do with him? I'll get my wagon and haul him home."

Paul sat up.

A silent, pale circle stood about them. On their knees beside him were Nancy and Jack.

"I'm all right," said Paul.

He climbed to his feet. With his great hands, Jack followed the movement, ready to support him if he should fall again.

But he would not fall again! He was stronger at that moment than ever he had been in the world. For he had come through the valley of death, and here was the face of lovely Nancy, pale, but lighted with eyes which were on fire with admiration.

CHAPTER IV

★

The First Lesson

There are various thresholds which we must cross, between that of life and that of death, and when young Paul Torridon had risen to his feet and stood safely on them, though his head still rang and his very soul was bruised by his great fall, yet he knew that he had crossed the greatest threshold of all and found himself.

He could look around upon that room without trembling. He went back to his desk, the huge Jack attending him. There, safely seated, he said in a rather faint voice: "Now we'll begin again—your names, please, on the slates."

Instantly the vast shoulders of Jack Brett bowed over the slate. He labored, and having finished, he turned slowly around and stared grimly about the schoolroom. There were a full half of the pupils who still had not entirely understood what change had occurred in the school, but the dreadful glare of Jack quickly convinced them that something had changed. They hastened to snatch at their pencils. There was no sight except that of bowed, earnest workers.

Then a little girl of eight began to cry.

"What's the matter?" asked the teacher.

"I dunno how to write," wailed the child. "My mummy never taught me!"

The head of Paul Torridon was quite clear now.

"Then I'll teach you," said he. "That's why I'm here."

He began to make a tour of the room and studied the sprawling and labored writings until he came to the slate of Nancy.

There he paused a moment.

"I think you had better be a teacher, too," said Torridon.

She looked quickly up to him, surprised, and then she flushed a little with pleasure.

"I will, if I can," said she.

He moved on and came to Jack Brett.

A certain rigidity about the back of the giant took his attention. The neck was as rigid as a pillar of red-hot steel. The head was poised to withstand shocks. And when he looked over the shoulder of the big fellow he saw upon the slate—a meaningless scrawl!!

He looked down into the eyes of Jack. They stared straight ahead. One who is about to enter the fire without protest would look forward in that manner.

Torridon picked up that slate and carried it to his desk, where he turned about and faced the class. Dreadful misery was in the face of big Jack now, and by the peculiar prescience of the sensitive soul, Paul understood what his late enemy expected—that the shapeless scratchings on his slate would be exposed to all eyes.

Torridon laid the slate upon his desk, face down.

"Jack Brett!" he said.

Jack Brett rose slowly to his feet. One hand was gripped into a fist, not to strike, but to endure.

"There's a lot of the wood in the shed that needs splitting. You'd better go and do that to-day."

Vast silence seized upon the school-room. They waited as for a thunder-bolt to strike. Then a faint sigh of amazement came from those who watched, for Jack Brett, his fine face crimson to the throat, turned and stalked from the room.

Still they waited, until from the rear of the school they heard the loud, crisp ring of an ax as it was driven home into hard wood. At that sound every eye in the schoolroom became empty, blank with submission, like the eye of a penned calf. Torridon knew that the great battle was fought and won.

All morning he worked. By noon he understood rather clearly what each in the room knew, and it was pathetically little. There was hardly a girl there who could not sew, spin, manage a creamery, cook. There was not a boy who could not bring one of the massive, soft-iron rifles to his shoulder and shoot a squirrel out of a treetop. But about books they knew little or nothing. Only Nancy knew.

To read, to write, to spell, to do arithmetic. Those were the tasks for which he must prepare them, and he went about it methodically, patiently, hopefully. Nancy helped at once. She took the little girls about her and started their small hands to work on the copies which she furnished them.

Noon came. Lunch was eaten. Then for a half hour the place echoed with shouts as the children played. And afterward, the long afternoon went by almost to dusk. For John Brett had set down the hours which the school should endure!

Many a weary, suffering face had Torridon to look at before the school was dismissed. He went to the door and thanked Nancy. If she would ask her father if he would permit her to help in the mornings, then in the afternoon he would teach her what he could.

"And how old are you, Nancy?"

"I'm fourteen."

He watched her go off after the others. He could tell her from the rest as long as she was in sight. Her clothes were as rough as those of the others, but she wore them differently. And her step was different. She was a harmony of pleasant music to Torridon.

Then the great shadow of Jack Brett stood before him.

"Well?" said Jack.

Torridon smiled frankly at him, though it was a twisted smile, for one side of his face was very swollen and sore.

"I thought it would be better if you stayed after school and worked with me," said he simply.

They sat by the stove. So long as the day lasted, Jack Brett worked. It seemed impossible that he should cramp down his big fingers enough to hold the pencil. He leaned his head low and grimly set his teeth. Gross were his untrained muscles, but in his mind there was the same steady patience which had made him, at twenty, the finest shot in all that close-shooting clan.

Afterward, they locked the door of the school. Dusk was falling. The blueness stood close at hand, with the frosty trees only dimly etched. The freezing ground crackled under their feet. For a moment they looked around at this. Then:

"Well, good night, Paul."

"Good night, Jack."

They separated and went home, but something more than words had passed between them. The thin legs of Torridon bore him lightly up all the way to the house and he found himself singing, though with a faint voice.

He soaked his swollen face with a cold compress, but it seemed as swollen as ever when he went in to supper and sat down at the great table. Curious glances fell on him. Little Ned, opposite him, stared frankly, as though at a stranger never before seen, and suddenly the great voice of John Brett boomed:

"Paul!"

He started to his feet. In that house every one rose when addressed by the master.

"Yes, sir," said Paul.

"What's happened to your face, eh?"

He had half expected that question. He had turned the answer in his mind half a dozen times. It was the expectation of that answer which had made Jack Brett so pale and grave when he said good-by that evening, for when the wrath of terrible John Brett descended upon the boy, it would be a thing to remember, to tell of in the clan for three generations.

He said slowly: "I had a fall to-day."

All heads lifted. All heads turned toward him. There was a peculiar wonder in every eye.

"You had a fall?" echoed John Brett in a voice of thunder. "Where?"

"On the ground," said Torridon.

"Come here to me!"

He went obediently, fear cold and heavy in his heart.

"You fell on the ground, did you?"

"Yes."

"What made you fall?"

Torridon was silent.

The voice of John Brett rose to a terrible thunder that shook the room.

"What made you fall?"

And still Torridon, cold and sick, was silent, and kept his eyes desperately fixed upon the eyes of the questioner. So he stood for hours of dread, as it seemed.

"Go back to your place!" said John Brett suddenly.

And Torridon went slowly back and sat down, stunned.

Opposite him he saw the malicious grin of Ned. Sly glances passed between the other boys. But only Aunt Ellen dared to speak, after a while, saying: "Standing up and defyin' the head of the house—that's what it's come to, eh? There's the Torridon in him speakin'!"

"Be quiet!" commanded John Brett.

Aunt Ellen raised her brows.

"I was teachin' him some manners," she muttered.

The tyrant growled: "*I'll* teach the young men of this house their manners. You—what've you been tryin' to do with Paul? Dress him up like a scarecrow? Ain't there enough clothes in this here house to dress him like—a man?"

It was a crushing blow for Aunt Ellen. Fiercely she scowled down at her plate, but her lord and master had spoken, and she dared make no reply. As for Torridon, he could not believe that he had heard correctly.

That meal ended. When the others filed out, he waited until the last, half expecting that the harsh voice of John Brett would summon him again, but no summons came. He was allowed to go free.

He went out to the barn. Every evening it was his habit to do that, and to slip into the big stall where Ashur was kept like a young prince. He had a feeling of possession in connection with that colt, for, having given it a name, and through it having come to some note in the house of the Bretts, he retained a sense of kindness toward it. So, in the worn darkness of the barn, he gave the colt a carrot and remained a moment while Ashur sniffed at him and nibbled at his pockets, in hope of something more. Like silk was the muzzle of Ashur, silken was the skin of his neck where the boy stroked it, and by degrees peace came slowly down upon Paul's soul, so troubled to-day, and so uplifted from the burden of the fear of man.

CHAPTER V

★

Patient And Perseverant

For several days he waited in expectation of punishment from John Brett, because he had stood before the king of the clan and refused to give an answer to his question, but the blow did not fall. And then, on the third day, Aunt Ellen clothed him in a new, stout homespun. John Brett viewed him with evident pleasure.

"Now you look like something," was all he said.

And the boy went off to his school.

Books had been ordered, books were arriving. Every evening young Torridon struggled eagerly ahead through the texts, making sure that he was perfect in them. For he himself must know before he could teach, and above all, there was the necessity of keeping well ahead of Nancy. She learned rapidly, smoothly. Her mind was like clear crystal, and imagined all things well. In the mornings she helped him with the little ones. In the afternoon, she was a careful student.

Discipline in that school was perfect. Jack Brett looked after it. There were two other hulking fellows almost as strong as Jack himself. He thrashed them both soundly before the first week was over, and after that the school went easily along. During that first strenuous week, Jack himself remained each evening to work at his writing. He carried home his slate. There he worked again, covertly, seriously, by lantern light, sitting up until the odd hours of the morning. But on the next Monday he could take his place regularly with the rest of the class.

He asked for no special treatment. Like a bulldog he fastened on his work, and gradually he improved. The example of well-disciplined industry which he exhibited worked well with the others. Small and big, they began to bend to their studies, and before Christmas came, big hands and small were writing and figuring to the great content of Torridon.

This occupation began to have its reaction upon him. He was no longer a wretched stray, to be scorned by the others. He had become a distinct person, and while no other youth among the clan of Brett would have looked forward to such a task as that of school-mastering, nevertheless Paul Torridon, being unique, was at least respected.

Sometimes he thought that some of their pleasure in his teaching was that they had made a member of another clan, an enemy, their servant, their public servant. But in the meantime, this new-found pride of spirit had even a physical reaction upon him. He grew taller, stronger. His cheeks no longer sank in beneath the cheek bones; there was a trace of hearty color in them. And, at Christmas time, another interest came into his life.

Big Jack, through all the weeks, had been rendering what service he could. Never once had he referred to the first tragic day in the school, nor to the shelter which the schoolmaster had put between him and the wrath of John Brett, but Torridon could feel that the big fellow's gratitude would never be exhausted.

Several times, at the noon hour and after school, he had offered to teach Torridon how to shoot. But the thin arms and the weak shoulders of Paul could not sway up the massive weight of a rifle and hold it steady. On the last day before Christmas, therefore, Jack had brought to the school a small package, and when the rest had gone from the school, he unwrapped his parcel and took out an old double-barreled pistol, made light and strong by some good gunsmith. He laid it in the hands of Paul Torridon.

"You can shoot this, Paul," he said. "Why, even a girl could handle it. It's like a feather!"

A feather indeed, in his great grasp, but to Paul Torridon it was weight enough. Nevertheless, when he closed his hand upon it, he felt that he had passed through another door and advanced still further into manhood.

There were tears of pleasure in his eyes when he shook hands with Jack. He accepted the small packet of powder and shot. Then Jack gave a little object lesson. He took the big chopping block as a target. Even then, standing not many paces away, he missed it thrice. The fourth bullet lodged in an upper corner, and Jack sighed with relief.

"A rifle's the gun for me," Jack said. "One of these here things, you gotta have nerves like steel to work with 'em. But you, Paul, you could do it. You—you can stand up and turn yourself into ice."

He flushed, making this oblique reference to the first day of school, when Paul had stood up only to be knocked down.

So Paul took his new treasure home.

He looked upon it as the most beautiful thing he had ever seen. The fact that big Jack had missed a target thrice with it showed that it was hard to master. But here was something within his strength, and once a master of the gun, then he would feel a man indeed!

It began a new period in his life. Excalibur to the young Arthur meant no more than this weapon to Paul Torridon.

The Indian border was not far away. The land was filled with rough men. The law of the land was not so strong as the law of guns, and this was a weapon which he could learn to use. He held it in an almost superstitious regard. Every night, his last act, performed with devotional care, was to clean it scrupulously, and through the day it never left him. Jack himself taught him how it could be carried out of sight in a sort of pouch under his left arm-pit, ready to be drawn. And it seemed that no one suspected that it was with him. Powder and lead were plentiful in the house of John Brett; what he took never was missed; and his practicing was done in the heart of the woods, where the small, hollow echo from the little weapon soon died away.

Yet the shooting of the gun was the smallest part of Paul's labor. He practiced for hours holding it on a mark. At first it twitched curiously in his nervous hand. But by degrees he learned to steady the nerves, until at last it was held in his fingers as in a rock.

In the three years that followed, he marked time by the progress which he made with the gun; and in the third year, when he walked toward the school over the frosted roads, woe betide the unlucky rabbit which tried to bolt across the way to shelter on the farther side. The pistol glinted into the hand of Torridon, and the rabbit leaped once, and leaped no more.

He had grown taller. Among the gigantic Bretts he was hardly more than a child, but actually he was well above the average. It was not in height that he differed from them so greatly, however, as in the manner of his making. There was hardly a woman or a girl among them with a hand so small, unless it was little Nancy's. There was hardly a pair of shoulders which would not have made two like his.

But he was not weak. He had not the power which enables a man to lug a heavy pack through the uncertain going of the woods for hours and hours, covering long miles. The lumbering giants of the Brett clan could do this. There was not a man of them who could not hold up his end. But Torridon, of a different blood, had other gifts.

If it came to a foot race—bare feet along the hard, beaten path—he flashed home by himself. Not even big Jack—now passed beyond John Brett's arbitrary school age—could keep up with the slender youngster. And that quality gave him additional standing, for fleetness of foot is prized in a community where speed of foot may mean the difference between life and death before the possessor is very old.

The massive rifle still was clumsy in his hands; he had an awe of it, but not fondness for its use, and therefore he was shut out from distinction in the most important of all backwoods pursuits. But he could ride a horse. He had no might to crush the ribs of a horse, as the Bretts were apt to do. He had no jaw-breaking power in his hands and arms to check his mount, either. But he learned that touch will do what power will not, and balance will keep the saddle when strong knees are flung to the ground.

So he grew up, light, wiry, nervously exact in his proportions. Beauty, after all, we are apt to judge by utility. In the backwoods, men wanted hands in which a massive ax would quiver like a reed, in which the ponderous iron rifle was a mere toy; to them such hands are beautiful. They wanted shoulders, too, which thought nothing of a hundred-pound pack and a day's march, in time of need. So such shoulders were a point of beauty, too. They wanted a body of sufficient bulk to match those vital hands and shoulders. So their ideal grew up as naturally as a tree from the ground. But if an artist had been there to scan them, and then turn his eyes to Paul Torridon, he would have had strange things to say, things of which Paul himself was most ignorant. He despised that slender, supple body of his, those quick, light hands. He despised all things about himself except, alone, his knowledge of books, which had made the clan prize him, and his ability with the pistol which, in some distant day, might come to mean much to him.

As for his attitude toward the clan, he accepted them because he knew nothing else.

Said Jack to him on a day—Jack, newly back from a long hunting trip, brown, hard, powerful as Hercules. "Tell me, Paul, don't you ever hanker to get over the mountains to your own people?"

Paul had often thought of it, of course. But his answer to himself always had been what it was to Jack Brett on this day: "Suppose that I started. They'd hunt me down with dogs, Jack."

"Who?" asked Jack, frowning.

"John Brett—your own father—perhaps you yourself, Jack!"

"I?" cried Jack. "Never, Paul!"

The school-teacher laid a hand on the arm of his great friend.

"You don't know yourself. Suppose that I'm out of sight. I'm no longer Paul. I'm just a Torridon. Well—what did they do to my people before me?"

Jack sighed and shook his massive head.

"I don't know, Paul," said he. "How do you know? It was a fair fight, I think."

"That's what the Bretts say."

"John Brett wouldn't lie."

"I'm afraid to ask him. Suppose he has to tell me an ugly

story? Then what would happen after that? He'd know that I hated him. He'd be suspicious. The first time I moved—that would be an end of me."

"But how can you stand it?" cried Jack. "Ain't you gunna try to find out?"

"Some day," nodded Paul.

"Well," said Jack, "you're—patient!"

And Torridon knew that an uglier word had been in the mind of his big friend.

CHAPTER VI

★

A Queen Dethroned

Yet it seemed to Paul the wise thing to wait and let time bring its own decision. Vaguely, little by little, he could feel manhood coming upon him. He could feel a strength—not the strength of a Brett—garbing him.

And at last that strength was revealed to all the clan and to him, as well.

Ashur, the beginning of his rise in the world, was the turning point again.

For John Brett, anxious that his chosen horse should grow great and strong, had refused to allow so much as a strap to be put on it until it came to its third year. And now, three years and more in age, he at last summoned the best rider he could find and bade him try out the colt.

Of course that was Roger Lincoln.

The great man came riding upon a lofty horse with rich wampum braided into its mane and tail. His own hair was free to flow down over his shoulders. He did not have a hat on his head. A crimson band around his forehead held the hair from fluttering into his eyes. Over his shoulder was a painted buffalo robe of price. He wore a splendid suit of antelope leather, beaded over almost its entire surface. His moccasins were miracles of Indian art.

Even when Paul Torridon saw him in the distance, with half a dozen fences in between to obscure him, he recognized Roger Lincoln by the many descriptions which he had heard of that glorious hero. For Roger Lincoln was a king of the prairies, far

West, and a true lord of the mind. Indian or white man, all were captivated by his mien, his grace, his dauntless heroism.

It was very lucky that John Brett could find him. Nine-tenths of his days were spent on the distant plains, but now he was back on one of his rare visits.

All the Bretts were on hand to see the breaking of Ashur.

That great event was to take place at ten in the morning. Hours before, the clan began to assemble at the house of John Brett and then poured out into the pasture. So the whole crowd turned when the coming of Roger Lincoln was announced.

He did not turn up the road. He came straight toward the pasture, jumping his horse over the fences on the way. It was a wonderful gray mare. Every one knew the story of how Roger Lincoln journeyed far south to the land of the Comanches and captured that mare, the pride of its horse-loving nation. It was not over tall, but it carried the weight of big Roger Lincoln like the merest feather, and winged its way over the fences, Roger Lincoln sitting handsomely at ease, his head high, his buffalo robe flaunting out behind him.

He seemed to be regarding distant things upon the horizon, paying no attention to the obstacles in his path.

So he came up to the pasture and leaped to the ground. With one hand he held the robe, flung gracefully about him. The other hand, his famous right hand, he offered to John Brett and to all the rest of the clan in turn, without making the slightest exception. He even paid that attention to tiny Miriam, two years old, as she backed against the knees of her mother and stared in fear at the tall stranger.

Paul Torridon followed that progress with interest. Every one seemed altered as by a touch of witchcraft at the coming of Roger Lincoln. The women seemed rudely made, ugly, clumsy, as he stood before them. The men, one after another, turned to heavy louts. Even Jack Brett, so tall, so handsome, so mighty of shoulder, seemed a staring, stupid boy in contrast with this bright Achilles of the plains.

There were only two exceptions, for even the coming of Roger Lincoln could not dim the fierce presence of John Brett, the patriarch and lawgiver. And when the hero came to Nancy Brett, although she was a small girl in her seventeenth year, she seemed to grow taller, older, more beautiful. Torridon himself, as he afterward knew, was seeing her for the first time, that instant. He had always felt, before, that she was a little too proud, too calm, too self-contained. If she were kind and gentle, often, it was merely because she had set herself a high standard and for the sake of her own self-respect she would not fall beneath that level. She was judicious, grave; there was nothing emotional about her, nothing free, easy, carefree.

But on this lovely day, when she took the hand of Roger Lincoln and smiled up into his handsome face, Torridon saw that there was an inner soul in Nancy such as he never had guessed at.

He was full of the wonder of this when Roger Lincoln approached him.

Of all the people gathered, Torridon was the only one that Roger Lincoln did not notice, and this was not because of any lack of courtesy on his part, but because Torridon was utterly overshadowed by the stallion.

He had been given the task of holding Ashur, and for a very good reason. The horse was not used to others. He had been treated with such scrupulous and almost frightened reverence by the rest of the clan, since the moment of his foaling, that no one dared to take liberties with him, fondle his arched neck, rub his forehead between his gleaming eyes. But Torridon had begun in the beginning. He had made his way with sugar and apples and carrots. It was he who groomed the proud young beauty every morning before he went to the school. It was he who whistled Ashur in from the pasture in the evening.

This morning, therefore, what more natural than that he should put the saddle on Ashur, and slip the bit between his teeth. He had taken Ashur by the forelock and pulled down his lofty head, so that the ear-stalls could be slipped into place.

Now, as the crowd gathered, it was Torridon who stood at the head of the stallion. He kept some wisps of grass with which to wipe away the froth that came as Ashur, growing excited in the presence of such numbers, champed at the bit and frothed.

And, while the observers circled and stared and wondered and admired this descendant of coal-black Nineveh, sometimes Ashur, wearied of them all, would close his eyes and flatten his ears, and thrust his nuzzle strongly against the breast of his keeper. At other times, however, he amused himself biting the backs of Torridon's hands. Sometimes he would catch the boy by the wrist and press harder and harder, mischievously dealing out pain until Torridon cried out in pretended agony. Then Ashur would throw up his glorious head, with upper lip stiffly distended, eyes wild, as though he expected a blow in repayment.

They were full of understanding of one another. For three years, they had known one another every day.

So it was only natural that Roger Lincoln, having made his circle of the crowd, when he came to the bright presence of the young stallion should not notice the youngster who stood at the head of the horse.

Roger Lincoln stood for a long time gazing. Silence came upon all the crowd. They were still with expectancy and fear, because Roger Lincoln, of course, knew horseflesh as no other man in the world could know it.

Only John Brett kept an unchanged face, but Torridon, who knew how to watch little things, made note that the pipe tilted up in the grip of the patriarch's teeth and from its bowl thick clouds of smoke were driven forth by his heavy breathing.

"Come here, Comanche," said Roger Lincoln.

The gray mare came to him like a dog, and all the women cried out softly, in admiration of such a tender intimacy between a man and his horse.

Then all fell silent again, biting their lips and looking from Lincoln to John Brett. Because, of course, it was patent that Roger Lincoln had some disagreeable things to say, but that he would not say them until he could illustrate the difference between the colt and a perfect pattern, such as the gray mare.

With a word the plainsman made his mare stand like a rock.

Then he began to circle the two. He stood behind them. He stood before them.

There was almost a tragedy when he reached for the hocks of Ashur. That young and haughty prince tried to bite and strike and kick at the same instant.

Torridon, blackness whirling before his eyes, looked to see Roger Lincoln fall torn and crushed to the ground, but the big man had slipped away, as a dead leaf slips from before a striking hand.

"I'll go with you," said Torridon eagerly. "Then he'll be all right."

"You will?" said Roger Lincoln, and he turned to Torridon and saw him for the first time.

Such eyes never had fallen upon Torridon before. They were between hazel and brown, and now they had a peculiar yellowish cast, like the eyes of a bird of prey.

"You're not afraid of him?" asked Roger Lincoln.

"He knows me," explained Torridon, and he stood beside the hip of the stallion and took him by the hock. The young stallion raised that leg and kicked with it, but it was only a small and feeble gesture that did not disturb Torridon's hold.

Roger Lincoln stepped up in turn, thus escorted, and laid his hand on the joint.

He fumbled at it for some moments. And, again escorted by Torridon, who was bursting with pride, the man from the Indian country thumbed and fingered the knee of Ashur, and the cannon bone beneath it.

Then he looked at the way the head was placed on the neck and put his fist beneath the jaws of the stallion while Torridon held Ashur irreverently by the nose.

At length the great man stepped back and looked at the gray mare and went over her, in turn, with as much care as he had used on the stallion.

When he had ended—and he had consumed a full half hour in this examination—"I haven't been on him, yet," he said to John Brett. "But from the ground I can tell you this. I've never seen the horse that compares with Comanche until to-day. And now I can tell you that he's as far above her as the sun is above the moon.''

John Brett blinked. There was a sort of moan of joy and relief from the others.

But Roger Lincoln laid his hand on the brow of the gray.

"Poor girl," said he. "Poor girl!"

It was as though a queen had been dethroned that day!

CHAPTER VII

★

Horse And Man

Torridon expected that the big man would, when he desired, simply leap into the saddle and gallop away on the colt. But he did nothing of the kind. First of all, he examined the girths with the greatest care and then looked to the straps. The saddle itself he seemed suspicious of, though it was new and strong. He took the measurement from his own stirrups and came back to lengthen these to the same degree. He looked well to the bit, the bridle, and above all to the reins.

Then he stepped back and said quietly to John Brett: "That colt may be spoiled. It's been petted too much!"

"Ha?" cried John Brett. "Paul Torridon, have you spoiled that horse with petting? I'll—"

He grew purple with rage; Paul Torridon grew white with fear.

"However," said Roger Lincoln, "it may turn out all right."

And he could not help a little smile, as though the sense of his own strength and skill overcame his modesty for an instant.

Then, in a trice, he had leaped into the saddle.

"Good boy!" he said gently to Ashur. "Go along. Get up!"

Ashur, as he felt the weight, turned stiff as a rock and crouched.

Torridon stepped back.

He forgot his fear of John Brett and began to grow hot with anger.

He knew very well that he had no right to feel this anger, but he could not help it when he saw Roger Lincoln on the back of Ashur.

"Get along!" said Roger Lincoln, and slapped the colt lightly on the flank.

Torridon could hardly keep back a voice that wanted to shout through his lips, tearing his throat with violence: "Don't do that! That's the wrong way! Let him go easily, give him time! He needs time to learn!"

Ashur, however, suddenly straightened and broke into a trot. It was wonderful to see the silken ease of his movement, the supple fetlocks playing under the strong drive of his legs.

From Roger Lincoln a single delightful glance flashed at John Brett. He pulled on the rein, and the colt swung slowly around while the crowd murmured: "Look! He's broken Ashur already! He's a perfect rider. What a man!"

Past John Brett came the colt, and Roger Lincoln leaned to say: "Brett, this horse is the king of the world!"

That instant Ashur acted as though he were a king indeed, and a very angry monarch.

He began to buck.

It was a coltish, clumsy beginning. He did not seem able to gather his legs under him, and he grunted when the weight of his rider beat relentlessly down on him.

Roger Lincoln laughed and kept a tight rein. With his free hand he slapped Ashur on the flanks.

"You might as well shake it out of yourself," he said.

That blow seemed to rouse a hornet's nest. Or perhaps it was that what Ashur had done before had been enough merely to warm his blood and give him a somewhat greater understanding of his powers. For now he went up into the air as though by the beat of wings, and he came down with head lowered, back humped.

The impact jarred the ground as far as where Torridon stood; and he could hear the gasp of breath driven from the body of Roger Lincoln by the shock.

But that was only the start. In that instant Ashur seemed to have learned all about bucking. He began to plunge high and come down on a stiffened foreleg, a double shock that snapped the head of Roger Lincoln heavily to the side, or down upon his breast. It was irresistible, like the snapping of a whiplash. And yet Roger Lincoln remained in the saddle!

"Ashur can kill himself, but he'll never get Roger Lincoln off," said some one.

Torridon turned his head.

It was Nancy who had said that, Nancy looking white and fierce, with her nostrils quivering. With wonder, Torridon saw that she was loving the battle.

He turned from her, a little sickened, in time to see Ashur spin like a top to the left, halt with planted hoofs that gouged up several feet of earth, and spin again in the opposite direction.

Then Roger Lincoln was flung from the saddle with incredible force.

His dignity dissolved in mid-air, so to speak. He was a whir of arms and legs, and then landed with a desperate thud, and rolled over at the very feet of Torridon.

Paul, looking down, knew by one glance at that white, senseless face and the half-open eyes that this man was badly stunned—killed, perhaps.

Then he heard a shout of men, with a tingling scream of women rising over it. People fled from about him, and there was Ashur coming like a tiger, with gaping mouth prepared to finish his victim.

"I spoiled him—I did it!" cried Paul to his own frightened, sorrowful heart.

And suddenly he was bestriding the fallen man and stretching out both his hands to ward off the resistless rush of the stallion.

"Ashur, you fiend!" he shouted.

The great, shining black body reared itself high above him. He was looking up into a gaping mouth from which the foam flew; and the eyes of Ashur were like the eyes of a dragon; and the mighty forehoofs of Ashur, each like a steel sledge in the hands of a giant, were poised to beat him to a lifeless pulp.

Even then Torridon had time to hear: "Don't shoot!" shouted in the great voice of John Brett.

Coward of the Clan ☆ 41

He had time to put the words together, added to an important thought—that his own life, even the added life of great Roger Lincoln, did not amount to the value of the life of Ashur, in the mind of John Brett.

Then the dreadful danger fell—but it swerved past him. The flying mane whipped his face with a hundred small lashes, and then the big horse swept away. He flaunted far off; he was a flash in the distance, with the reins tossing high above his neck.

A wave of people spilled around them. They brushed Paul aside, for of course the question was simply: What had happened to Roger Lincoln?

Torridon sank down beside a stump of a tree which marred the surface of the green pasture. He felt nauseated. When he opened his eyes the landscape spun violently. When he closed his eyes it spun with still more fury. And he felt sweat running down his face in rivulets of ice.

Voices sounded in the distance—how far in the distance they were; how hollow! They broke slowly, the sound vibrations rolling up through his body and roaring in his ears. Those were the voices of people thronging around Roger Lincoln.

At length they had picked him up and were departing toward the house. Women were scampering ahead, holding up their skirts so that they could run more rapidly. In the midst of his dizziness Paul looked after them and almost laughed, they were so like waddling ducks.

A shadow crossed him; some one dropped upon knees beside him.

"Were you hurt, Paul?" asked the voice of Nancy Brett.

It jerked one veil of darkness from his eyes and he looked up at her, amazed. She looked anxious and white. Her lips were parted.

"How is Roger Lincoln?" asked Torridon. "I think he broke his neck."

"I don't know," said Nancy. "Do you feel pain, Paul?"

"I seemed to hear it!" muttered Torridon. "I seemed to hear the bone snapping—"

He clutched his face with one hand.

"Did Ashur strike you with one of his feet?" asked Nancy. "Try to tell me, Paul!"

"He—he fell right before me, Nancy!" gasped Torridon.

"I don't care!" cried she. "I want to know about you. Did he strike you?"

She began to pass her hands over his head. Her fingers were trembling.

"I'm all right," gasped Torridon. "But I feel awfully sick."

"You'd better lie flat. Keep your eyes closed," she ordered.

She took him by the shoulders and pushed him down. He tried to resist her.

"I don't want to be a baby. They'll think I fainted," protested Torridon, but as he tried to struggle, a shuddering dissolved his strength and he collapsed on the ground.

She sat close beside him. With a handkerchief she wiped his face. Then she began to fan him.

"Put out your hands and take hold of the grass," she said.

He obeyed.

"Is that better?"

"Yes, Nancy. It's—it's—"

"You don't have to talk. Just lie still. Just close your eyes."

He obeyed.

Presently he said: "I can feel the strength coming back."

"You'll be all right in a moment more. Your color's a lot better. It's the touch of the ground that helps. I know!"

"No, it's coming from you into me; the strength, Nancy, I mean. I think I can sit up now."

"You'd better not."

"I don't want them to see me like this. I'd rather die than have them see me."

"There, I'll help."

She drew him up and put his shoulders against the stump of the tree. He could open his eyes. The landscape no longer was spinning, and in the distance the stallion was grazing.

"Who wanted to shoot? Was it Jack?"

"Yes."

"Dear old Jack!"

Weak tears ran into his eyes.

"You'd better go away, Nancy," he murmured, and he looked down with bent head lest she should see his trembling lip and the water in his eyes.

She said simply: "Uncle John wouldn't let him shoot. He— he thought the horse was more—Paul Torridon, you're crying like a baby!"

"I can't help it! Nancy, please, please go away!"

She stood up. He heard the rustling of her dress as she left him.

CHAPTER VIII

★

Paul and Ashur

Afterward he could sit on the stump, though he still was weak in the knees and in the elbows. He wished with all his heart that he had not seen the bright face of Nancy when she spoke to Lincoln that day, because if he had not, he would not have cared for her opinion so much, but now he felt dreadfully disgraced. He was a man, and he had cried at the thought of the goodness of Jack Brett.

So, clasping his hands together and tearing them apart again, he sat in suffering.

Some one came out from the house toward him. It was Charlie Brett, who of all the young men in the clan had the least good feeling for him, since they lived in the same house. Young men cannot be near one another without forming a great attachment or a profound dislike. There is no such thing as indifference.

First the idea came to the mind of the school-teacher that Nancy must have told Charles and that he had come to mock a grown man who cried like a girl.

So Torridon stood up and began to walk up and down. He made himself whistle, though he did not know the tune which puckered his lips.

But when Charlie came up he said in a respectful tone: "Dad wants to know will you come into the house, Paul? Roger Lincoln wants to talk to you."

Torridon, in duty bound, went toward the house, and Charlie went beside him, though at a little distance, for he kept his head

Coward of the Clan ☆ 45

turned toward Torridon and watched him with an intensity of awe, like a child viewing a strange monster in a cage.

Torridon was more ill at ease than ever when he came into the house. He knew that many of the methods of John Brett were terrible. Now he might choose to shame him before the entire household. He was convinced something dreadful would happen when he found that almost the whole clan was gathered in the big central room of the house. There was Roger Lincoln, reclining in John Brett's own chair, and John Brett stood beside him, looking more fierce, more sage, more patriarchal than ever before.

When Torridon came in with his light step, in place of the universal indifference which usually greeted him, he found that all heads turned suddenly toward him, and all eyes remained fixed upon him.

They were all waiting.

He halted near the door and waited, too, tense and white, praying that the trembling in his heart might stop. But it did not stop. It grew greater. There was not even a whisper of sound. All stared at him except Roger Lincoln, who was looking down at the floor, his long hands folded in his lap.

Paul glanced around him. Yonder was Nancy Brett—the traitor who had told of his weakness. He thought at first that her faint smile was mockery, now; but then he saw that her eyes were big and tender.

Roger Lincoln looked up. He held out his hand. His handsome face lighted with a smile.

Irresistibly drawn, Torridon went up to him.

His fingers were taken in that strong and gentle clasp.

"Out yonder among the plains Indians," said Roger Lincoln, "they have a habit of showing their friendship by giving you a tepee and everything that's in it—by giving you an entire string of horses—by offering you their rifles and the scalps they've taken."

He paused, still smiling.

"White men can't offer things like that. It's too much like buying friendship. What I can say is that I love my life, Torridon. No one has a better time than I do; no one loves his life more. Well, you've saved it for me. To be killed by a horse? Bah! That's worse than to die at the hands of Sioux! But, at any rate, I want to offer you before these people—so they'll be witnesses if ever I break my word—I want to offer you my hand and everything that I have—my gun, my horse, my money, my heart, Torridon. I'm going to leave in a few moments, if I can ride. As to the black colt, you're the man to handle him. I should have seen that at the first. In the meantime, if you ever should need me, send after me. This is my mother's ring, and I'll always go back with the bearer of it to find you."

Torridon took it, feeling himself turn from cold to hot. He could not speak. There was not a word in the world that he could bring into his mind.

Then John Brett said: "The lad's lost his tongue. But he feels what you say, Lincoln. He's a good lad."

That covered Torridon's retreat as he stumbled back into the throng.

Or rather, he tried to get into it and hide himself, but he could not. They drew back from him a little in order that they could see him. Only old Aunt Ellen came and plucked at his arm with fingers like steel claws.

"The heart is the biggest half of the man," said Aunt Ellen, and cackled at him like a hen.

He moved away. He found a door and escaped.

All the world was new, delightful, gentle, bright. He moved in an ecstasy the more violent because he felt that the appreciation he had met with was undeserved. It was something for nothing. His weak tears, surely, had more than balanced that withstanding of the stallion's rush. But they were not noticed. Nancy had not said a word.

He went into the trees near the house and waited there, hot with joy, ashamed of seeing the faces of his fellows, until he saw Roger Lincoln depart, riding as straight as ever, but keeping gray Comanche at a walk. No doubt he was dreadfully hurt and shaken by his fall, but no one would have guessed it, except that the dashing rider went now so slowly. The heart of Torridon swelled with admiration and worship.

That was a man!

Some of the young men followed Roger Lincoln, making an escort for him, as befitted his dignity, but all the others came back into the pasture near by. He saw several of the youngsters sent off by John Brett. Then the voice of the patriarch himself was raised:

"Paul! Oh, Paul! Paul Torridon!"

He came slowly out of the wood and toward them. They had smiles for him. They drew back and opened a lane to where John Brett was standing.

"Sneaked off and hid yourself, eh?" said that giant. "You act like a girl, pretty near, Paul. Now, we all come here to-day to see Ashur rode. Are you gunna disappoint us?"

Paul blanched as he thought of the plunging black monster and the form of Roger Lincoln hurtling through the air.

"Go get that hoss and ride him here!" roared John Brett.

And the force of his voice blew Torridon away.

He crossed the pasture with shaking knees, but when he was near, the stallion saw him and came trotting and tossing his head in the unaccustomed bridle.

He had broken the reins. Torridon was glad of it and of the little delay which this excused as he knotted them securely once more. Ashur in the meantime was hunting at his pockets for carrots. And, finding none, he transferred his attention to Torridon's head and began to push his hat about.

He merely turned his head curiously when Torridon put foot in the stirrup. But, when he drew himself off the ground, Ashur grunted and flinched away.

"Heaven help me!" thought Torridon.

But he was able to throw his leg over the saddle, and by kind fortune it fell exactly in the opposite stirrup.

Ashur, sprawled in a most awkward position, was reaching about and biting at the knee of his new rider. So Torridon in a shaking voice, reassured him.

"Get on!" whispered Torridon. "Good boy Ashur! If ever

I've given you carrots and apples, be a good horse to-day to me!''

Ashur tossed his head and walked a few steps.

A shout of triumph rang from the far side of the pasture and Ashur leaped a dozen feet sideways in acknowledgment of it. But Torridon, braced and ready, was not unseated.

He kept the lightest touch on the reins. He made no effort to control Ashur; he merely wanted Ashur to control himself. And the colt turned his head again with a mulish expression, one ear back and one tilted forward.

Then, unbidden, he broke into a gallop; he bounded high into the air and a groan echoed heavily over the field—an expression of the boy's heart, though spoken by the crowd. Yet he kept his seat by balance only, and with the reins he barely kept in touch with the stallion letting him have his head freely, but always talking softly, steadily.

Ashur suddenly began to fly. He had been galloping fast before, but this gait had wings to it. He headed straight for the fence.

"A crash!" thought Torridon, and set his teeth and tried to hope for heaven.

Ashur rose like a bird, floated, landed lightly, and went on in his stride.

Oh, noble Ashur! The heart of the boy began to rise.

They flew through the soft meadow beyond. Ashur was loving this run! They reached the brook and, soaring high, the stallion cleared it and sped on beyond while Torridon shouted with a sudden joy. Fear had been snatched away from him. He understood now. To Ashur it was merely a frolic and the stallion rejoiced to have his old companion with him.

He pulled on the right-hand rein. The head came first. But then, understanding, Ashur curved with the pull and swung back. Once more the silver face of the creek shot beneath them. They winged the fence to the pasture, and now, at the draw of both reins, Ashur fell to a canter, to a trot, to a walk, and came to a stop fairly before John Brett.

A shout of triumph rang up again. Ashur leaped and whirled

at the same time and Torridon found himself sitting on the ground. There had been hardly a jar. The colt simply had twitched from beneath him.

"You fools!" groaned John Brett. "You've spoiled the chance with your yapping! Silence, there! Catch the horse, some of you."

There was no need, for Ashur came quickly back and sniffed at the shoulder of Torridon and stood like a rock, then, while Torridon sprang up and into the saddle again.

"He didn't mean it," said Torridon. "He goes like an old horse, without a fault. Look!"

And he began to ride Ashur in a figure eight before them all, at a trot, at a walk, at a canter.

CHAPTER IX

★

All For A Torridon

There had been three steps in the climbing of the ladder. Now, dizzy with joy, Paul Torridon found himself at the top—the most considered youth in the clan of which he was not a member.

That very night John Brett grew tired of bellowing the length of the table. He had Torridon come up and sit beside him, where they could converse about horses in general and, particularly, of that horse which was nearest to the heart of John Brett. He urged Paul to waste no time in other pursuits. The perfect breaking of the stallion so that even a child would be at home on his back was the thing for him to do now.

For a month Torridon had no other occupation. Except that he slept in the house, he was with Ashur every moment. He groomed him in the morning, fed him, watered him. Then exercise in the fresh cool of the day. Then a thorough rubdown and drying out. Then freedom in the pasture, where the teacher followed.

He was intent on rewarding John Brett for the home and the shelter which had been given to him by making an absolute masterpiece of this work which had been given into his hands. The patience which he had acquired during his wretched childhood and the added patience which he had gained by slowly grinding knowledge into the heads of young Bretts whose brains were befogged with too much outdoors now helped him in training the horse.

Already much had been done. Ashur had known the whistle and the voice of his master. He had formed the habit of absolute

Coward of the Clan ☆ 51

trust and confidence in Torridon, and when an animal believes that a man can do no wrong, nine-tenths of the battle is over. But there were other things which had to be taught, many of them; and though Ashur was a wonderfully adroit equine pupil, still the alotted month was a short time.

A month to give a horse perfect manners.

But Torridon would not be contented with that. He worked by day and he worked by night. A nervous horse would have gone mad under the coaching which this one received, but the nerves of Ashur were as steady as steel. He could have lessons for endless hours, and still take them with lightness as though they were a game.

So, one month from that first riding of the colt, John Brett and twenty others turned out to see the riding. They expected to see a fairly broken horse; they saw, instead, a masterpiece of manners.

Torridon sat in the saddle with shining eyes. He had groomed Ashur until the black velvet of his skin seemed black no longer, but flashing silver metal wherever the sun touched. Moreover, there was a change in the very physique of Ashur. A month of steady work had taken the foolish colt look out of his eyes, and the muscles were beginning to show like ropes along his thighs and shoulders. His belly was stiff with heavy power; his quarters were beginning to be defined more square and precise. From just behind, he looked strong enough to pull a plow!

With an audience to look on, Torridon rode Ashur up and down. There was no tugging at the reins, until he asked the stallion for a burst of speed which needed a bit of a pull for steadying. Ashur walked, trotted, cantered, raced. He was drawn from one pace down to another, flung from one pace into high speed again.

When Torridon checked him at last, John Brett laughed with pleasure.

"Stove polish couldn't finish him no finer, Paul," he admitted. "Now let one of the boys take him."

"There's something more," urged Torridon.

And, looping the reins over the pommel, he folded his arms

and controlled the stallion by the mere sound of his voice. He started, stopped, increased speed, slowed, swerved right and left slowly, dodged right and left as though confronted by sudden anger.

Again he halted. And a good hearty shout of applause was sweet in the ears of Torridon. Even the young men joined in. For though they would have been envious of most feats of horsemanship, they felt that this youngster had risen to a class so high that he could be admired from a distance. They raised a whoop with the others, so that a crowd of crows, startled from the trees, flapped heavily away into the distance.

"There's something more," said Torridon, bursting with his pride.

Once more the reins were dropped upon the pommel, and this time Ashur went through his paces guided neither by hand nor voice. Pressure of heel or hand or sway of body accomplished all those effects. Indeed, it was not so very unusual an accomplishment. More than one plainsman had taught his favorite mount to leave his hands and voice free in the time of need. But the manners of Ashur were such a vivid contrast to those which he had possessed only a few weeks before that the watchers hardly could believe their eyes.

And to crown all, bringing the stallion back before John Brett, at an unseen signal, Torridon made him kneel, then fling himself prostrate on his side, while the rider stepped easily to the ground.

There was no need to explain the advantage of that last trick. All who might have to use their horses as breastworks in the desert against Indian attack appreciated it.

A single gesture, and Ashur sprang to his feet, shaking himself like a dog, while his bridle rang.

"Mount, Charlie," said John Brett. "We'll see how Ashur goes with another."

Charlie Brett came with shining eyes, pleased to be mentioned even by his father, and eager to show how he could sit the saddle.

The stirrups were altered a little to suit him; then he sprang up.

Coward of the Clan ☆ 53

Ashur stood like stiff iron, his ears flattened.

"Get down," said Torridon anxiously. "Get down, Charlie! He means trouble! He means trouble! Get down!"

"Stand away from his head," answered Charles Brett with perfect assurance. "If I can't ride this hoss now, I can't ride a stick. He's broke as smooth as silk."

"Uncle John," begged Torridon, for so they all termed the head of the clan, "make him get down. Ashur looks dangerous."

"Stand away," answered John Brett. "It ain't any shame to you if somebody else can ride the hoss that you've trained so slick. Let's see him run, Charlie!"

Charlie, nothing loath, leaned in the saddle, gripped hard with his knees, and tightened the reins. He had no time or need to give a starting touch of his heels. As Torridon stepped back, Ashur leaped. He was in the middle of the pasture before the first gasp of the spectators began.

Then something happened. Even Torridon, watching every instant in fear, could not be sure. The black horse seemed suddenly to be in two places at once, so swiftly did he dodge and double, and Charlie sailed from the saddle and rolled over and over on the ground.

He came to his feet again with a shout of terror, running for his life, and with good reason, for the stallion was about and after him with tigerish eagerness.

"Shoot!" screamed a woman.

The whistle of Torridon went like a needle through the air. The stallion tossed his head and, swerving from the fugitive, came back in a broad sweep toward the crowd. They scattered with cries of fear as though they expected him to crash straight through them.

But Torridon was his goal, and before his master he stopped, mischief still hot and bright in his eyes, stamping and dripping from exercise.

John Brett lowered the rifle which he had just raised. He turned to Torridon with a grave face.

"Paul," he said, "I'll not forgive you if you been making that a one-man hoss!"

Torridon could not answer. The peril in which Charlie had been placed, and his own astonishment, stifled him, and he stared helplessly back at the patriarch.

"Jack!" called John Brett. "We'll make this thing sure, now. Jack, will you take a chance in that saddle?"

Jack, pale but determined, came from the crowd, settling his hat more firmly on his head.

"Go with him," cautioned John Brett.

But as Jack mounted, Torridon already was hurrying to the side of his friend.

"Take him easily—talk to him!" he cautioned. "I don't know what's in him! He's never tried anything like this with me!"

Jack spoke, indeed, but his quiet voice had no effect on the big black. Ashur stood trembling, ready to spring into the air. He kept turning his proud, fierce head to Torridon, thrusting at his shoulder with his nuzzle as though asking impatiently why this indignity should be.

"I'll try him now," said Jack, and turned the head of the colt well away from its teacher.

The trial lasted not half a second. Two whiplash leaps and stops dropped Jack as though he had been struck from the saddle by a club, and the stallion wheeled at him furiously, always intent to kill.

The horrified cry of Torridon stopped him; he came back to Paul and danced like a savage panther behind him, looking over his shoulder at the world and champing foam from his bit.

Jack staggered to his feet and stood straight.

"He turned into a steel cable on springs," said Jack quietly. "And then somebody got hold of the far end of the cable and cracked it a couple of times under me."

He smiled, but his eyes were still blank with the shock which he had received.

Back they went to John Brett and the murmuring, horror-stricken crowd.

"I'll teach somebody to handle him," protested Torridon eagerly. "I know that with time I can do it."

John Brett smiled bitterly.

"I spent half my life at the breeding of that hoss," he said with unbreakable gloom. "And now it sort of looks like I'd done all of that work for a Torridon."

He turned on his heel and walked toward the house, and for the first time in many months Torridon felt the gulf open at his feet. He was a Torridon; they were Bretts. Nothing on earth could heal the breach.

CHAPTER X

★

None So Blind

Autumn and the school year were at hand now, but Torridon worked feverishly through the interim to try to teach one member of the household to back the stallion with safety. Charlie was the willing pupil. To Charlie he taught the whistle, the call; to Charlie he taught the tricks of guiding without reins, by voice, by gesture and signal, by sway of the body.

It was utterly of no avail.

Released from the hand of his master, the black colt was a tiger instantly. Twice a serious mauling of Charlie was barely averted, and Charlie gave up the effort. John Brett, when this was explained to him, smiled, half sadly, and half in anger. But he spoke no more about the colt. One might have thought that Ashur was no more to him than a shadow of a horse.

But Torridon knew better, and watching that stern, cold face, he saw that he had outworn his welcome among this clan of his enemies. The court takes its tone from the king; all eyes fell coldly upon him, except the eyes of Nancy and those of Jack.

Those two, stanch as oak, did not alter. One day Jack stopped at the house with word that Nancy wanted to see him.

"She's gone out riding up Bramble River. You'd catch her along that road, Paul, if you rode Ashur."

Paul saddled Ashur in haste.

The way to the Bramble River led through a semicircle of trails and roads, but with Ashur it was possible to go cross-country like a bird. There was sadness in the heart of Torridon as he went, for it might be the last day he backed the stallion.

Coward of the Clan ☆ 57

At any moment he expected from John Brett the command never to go near the black colt again.

They reached the river road at last. It was not really a road. No one ever had leveled it, but strong wagons had been dragged along its course more than once, and where wheels once had traveled, it was the custom to speak of a road. It was in reality merely a winding hint of a trail, twisting back and forth among the trees. Then Paul saw a rider before him, a woman. He called to Ashur, and the stallion swept up to her like the wind.

She had turned to face them, laughing with pleasure at the speed of the horse. Laughing more than a little, felt Torridon, at his own eagerness.

"You wanted me, Nancy?"

"Let's sit down," said Nancy. "There's a rock by the water. And Ashur's such a silly fool. He's always dancing."

They tethered Nan's gelding to a tree. Ashur, certain not to stray, was turned loose, and the two sat on a table-topped rock at the verge of the river. Their feet were on sand as clean and white as the sand of a sea beach. The broad river swept before them. Moving water hypnotizes. Torridon began to feel that they were on an island together—then that the island had broken adrift and was sweeping out into the stream.

Nancy had not spoken. He looked at her presently, startled. He found that she was smiling with thoughtful eyes.

"You'd forgotten that I was with you, I think," said she.

"Oh, no," said he, and turned a brilliant red, thereby confessing.

"Well," said Nancy, nodding. "That's books. They take you away from things."

He looked at her with frightened eyes. She was so practical and so full of common sense, often, that he was in awe of her. She differed from the others of the clan. They simply could understand nothing but the earth and things of the earth. That vague, cloudy universe in which he lived they never entered. But Nancy could enter it, if she chose. She knew all about it, he felt, and she wanted none of it. She preferred facts, it seemed. He respected Nancy, and her beauty delighted him, but he was afraid of her. He always had been afraid of her, from the first day when he met her judicial eyes in the school.

"Yes," he said vaguely.

She shrugged her shoulders.

"I wanted to talk to you about yourself," said Nancy.

Paul sat up straight. He picked up a stick and jabbed it nervously into the strip of white sand.

"Don't do that," said Nancy. "You're making the mud show through."

He threw the stick away with a nervous gesture and clasped his hands together.

She went on: "What are you going to do with yourself, Paul?"

"I don't know," said he. "I don't know what you mean, exactly."

"Just what I say. For instance, what are you going to do this winter?"

"Teach the school, of course."

"How old are you, Paul?"

"I'm nineteen. That makes you eighteen, doesn't it?"

"Do you know that much about me?"

She laughed a little, nodding to herself, laughing at him. And he flushed again. Color always was coming and going in his pale face with every emotion.

"You won't teach the school, though," said she, "if you're wise."

"And why, Nan?"

"Because you're a Torridon," she said bluntly.

She frowned, driving home her point with cruelty.

"I've always been a Torridon."

"Different, though."

"Just as much before."

"You were only a boy. Children don't count so much."

"I'm not so very old now," said Torridon anxiously.

"You're a great deal older than you think."

"Why do you say that?"

"You're always looking forward, thinking that you're going to grow bigger."

"I didn't think you'd taunt me with that," said Torridon, straightening his shoulders and growing crimson with shame and sorrow.

"Don't be silly. I don't mean your size. You're big enough. I only mean—in your mind. You keep thinking that you'll change. Perhaps you will. You feel like a child, now, compared to what you hope to be. But the Bretts don't see things that way. When a boy has his height, he's a man. We'll, you're a man to us!"

He was silent. There was so much truth in what she said that he could not answer. He was depressed. One always is downhearted when it appears that another knows the truth about one. Conversation flows out of mysteries, half knowings, partial revealings of what is kept securely hidden, more securely hidden because it is half revealed.

"I'm just the same as I was last year," said he.

"You're not, though," she replied with her usual assurance.

"What's made the difference?"

"That!"

She pointed to Ashur.

"Speak to him," she said.

"Ashur!" said he.

The stallion jerked up his head and looked on his master with bright eyes of love and trust.

"That's made the difference," said the girl.

He shook his head, bewildered.

"I mean, when you were a boy, it didn't matter. But after you mastered the school, and big Jack—"

"I didn't master Jack."

"What did happen, then?" she asked sharply, still frowning at him. "Don't talk small, Paul, to make me talk big about what you've done!"

"I think you're a little rude," said Paul Torridon, so angry and proud that he was about to spring to his feet and leave her.

"Nonsense," said the girl. "You're very hard to handle. You're just like—a girl!"

He did leap up, then.

"I think I'll go home," said he.

She answered calmly: "What home?"

"Why, to Uncle John's place, of course."

"He's not your uncle."

Torridon tried to answer. He could not, and because he was unable to find a word he began to hate Nancy.

"And his house isn't your home, Paul!"

"Is that what you brought me here to tell me?"

"Just exactly," said Nancy. "When you were a child, that was different. Then you changed into a youngster. You showed that you had something in you when you turned Jack into a sort of—slave to you."

"Slave? What are you talking about, Nancy? You're just—you're just trying to make me angry."

"What else is he?" said the girl. "Does he do anything without coming to you for advice? Does he ever think anything out for himself? Look at last year. He wanted to marry Charlotte. He went to you, and you told him he'd better save a lot of money first, and build a cabin before he married her. So she got tired of waiting and married Will Morgan."

The dreadful truth of this was dropped upon him, a load that bowed his shoulders.

"I thought it was best," he said stiffly.

"Perhaps it was best. That's not the point at all. You'd better sit down, Paul."

"I think maybe I'm needed back at the house," replied Paul.

"No, you're not!"

"See here, Nancy. Don't you talk like this any more," he cried at her. "I won't listen. You're just trying to upset me."

Nancy stamped lightly on the sand. It made a crisp sound under her foot.

"You—you baby!" cried Nancy. "You won't dare to open your eyes and see facts. You're afraid of the truth!"

He braced himself, actually planting his feet to withstand the shock.

"What truth?" he asked her.

"That you've turned into a man—that the whole lot of us knew it the day you saved Roger Lincoln. Saved Roger Lincoln—think of that! And then you rode Ashur yourself! We knew that day that you were a man. We knew that you were a Torridon. We began to hate you from that minute, and you're afraid to see it. You won't see it or admit it till somebody shoots you through the back."

CHAPTER XI

★

By The River's Brim

He sat down, not because he felt more kindly toward the girl, or because he was more prepared to listen to the truths which she was telling him, but because her last words had tapped him behind the knees and unstrung the sinews, so to speak.

He began to fumble at his cold face with one hand, flashing glances at her, and then at the brightness of the river.

She sat bolt upright, with her head high, looking straight at him.

"You *do* hate me, I see," said Torridon.

"Is your lip trembling?" she asked, coldly and sternly.

"Oh, Nancy," he exclaimed, "how can you be so brutal?"

"I can't be brutal to you," she said. "I'm only a weak girl. And you're a strong man!"

He opened his eyes at her. He parted his lips.

"A strong man?" he repeated. Then he laughed bitterly and added: "You're wicked enough to keep taunting me, too!"

She exclaimed with impatience.

"I suppose I have to prove it to you!" she said. "What do you mean by strength?"

"Oh, Nancy," sighed the boy, "does it give you pleasure to show you that I know? Well—there you are—look at them—look at my hands!"

He flung them out before her—slender, delicately made hands.

"Well," she said, "suppose you had big hands. What could you do with them?"

Coward of the Clan ☆ 63

He laughed bitterly and jerked up his head. "I could—well, I could throw logs around as if they were matchwood."

"Humph!" said Nancy.

"I could—I could knock down a bull!"

"Like Jack, you mean?"

"Yes, yes. Oh, what a man Jack is!"

"And who is Jack's master?" she said.

"Don't talk like that, Nancy. Of course I'm not his master."

"You are, you are!" said she.

"This is just saying 'yes' and 'no' like children. You can believe that, if you want to."

"Who is the strongest man that ever came among us—the bravest, most wonderful man?"

"Do you mean Roger Lincoln?"

"Of course I mean Roger Lincoln."

"Yes," nodded the boy with interest.

"Well, then, who was it that got the affection of Roger Lincoln when he came? Who was it that became a sort of brother to Roger Lincoln? Which of the strongest men in the clan?"

"That?" murmured Paul. "That was just a sort of accident."

"Does Roger Lincoln like weak men?" she asked sharply. "Is he a fool? Does he offer his friendship forever to fools and weaklings?"

Torridon was agape.

Then he said slowly: "I can't carry a pack the way they do, Nan. My legs buckle under the weight."

"Horses are for carrying packs," said she.

"If I wrestle—even the youngsters can throw me down."

"Partly because you don't put any heart into it. You take it for granted that you'll be beaten. Besides, men don't fight with wrestling—they don't fight with bare hands."

"They fight with rifles!" he exclaimed. "And what am I with a rifle? They're too heavy for me!"

"You haven't tried one for years. You know you haven't. You could handle a rifle now just as well as any one."

He started to deny this, but hesitated. It was true that he had not made the attempt for a long time.

"You just give up," said the girl. "You just sit and wring your hands like an old woman. But you have a pistol."

He started.

"Jack told you that?"

"Yes. Jack tells me everything. Look! Could you hit that with your pistol?"

She picked up a pebble and tossed it a dozen yards away.

"Perhaps," he said.

He drew the pistol and fired. The pebble disappeared.

Then he began to reload, absentmindedly, never looking at his gun.

"Well," said the girl after a moment, "who else among us could do that?"

"What does a pistol matter?" he said sadly.

"Suppose that pebble had been the heart of a man?" said the girl.

"I never thought of that," muttered he.

Then he added: "Well, what do you want me to do?"

"Leave us while you have a chance to leave. While you have life in you!"

"You don't think they'd murder me, Nancy? Why should they want to? What have I ever done to them?"

"You've stolen Ashur."

"No, no, no! I wouldn't dream of doing it!"

"You don't understand. You have to hear it in words of one syllable, I suppose. Well, why do wolves kill a dog?"

"Why, because—because they're different, and—"

"That's why the Bretts will kill you. Because you're different. You're a Torridon." She went on, gravely: "There's not a man or a woman in the tribe who likes you, except Jack. There's not one that doesn't hate you, really; or they would hate you, if any one encouraged them to do it. The young men are jealous of you. The girls don't understand you. They think you despise them because you never go near them."

"But, Nancy, how crazy that is! I'm simply afraid of them!"

"Well, I've told you what you ought to know."

He dropped his chin on his hand. After a while he could hear the rustling of the water; again, the noise of the horses, grinding the grass with their powerful jaws.

"Now, Paul, tell me just what's in your mind this very minute."

"I—a great many things."

"I want to know exactly what you're seeing and thinking and hearing."

"How all the gold and red and purple from the trees and the bushes floats in the stream there. It never is drowned, Nancy. Nothing that's real seems to be worth while. Do you see?"

"I don't see. Why do you look at the trees in the water, and not on the bank, just opposite, and all around us?"

"Well, those trees will lose all their leaves the first strong wind that comes along. But their images in the water—you see where the still water is, around the curve?—they stand in the water taller and bigger and brighter than they really are. You can see the blue of the sky, too, and a bright streak of cloud all filled with sun. That's not real, so you can look at that picture in the water and it will never die. It's like a thought. You see that, Nancy?"

She nodded and muttered something.

"There is no wind to go moaning and mourning through the branches that are reflected there, Nan. That's important, I think. Now, while I look at that picture, I'm hearing all the humming and buzzing and whirring and singing of the insects: the hornets, and the wasps, and the bumblebees and the bees, and the crickets and the flies, and the grasshoppers. They aren't real noises. If you speak you put out all those sounds. Well, you see how it is. You just sit close to the ground with your eyes and your ears open, and you gather things in. All those things die. They're singing just for this autumn only. Two days together the sounds will never be the same singing exactly. So it's better to shut your eyes on things as they are and see them as you want them to be."

"That's all I wanted to know," said Nancy briskly. "I've told you that you're in danger of your life and you start in thinking about reflections in the water, and humming bees. I'm finished,

Paul. I'll never try to do anything for you again! I just suspected that it would be like this."

"You want me to go away," said he, looking deep in the quivering beauty that lay in golden towers inlaid with blue in the river. "Well, I would have to leave Ashur if I went."

"A man can live without a horse," said she. "Besides, you'll have your memory of Ashur, you know. And memories and thoughts, they're all that you really care about."

He was so earnestly intent that he failed to see the sarcasm.

"Oh, no, they're not; not always, I mean. There's Ashur. I can't use him for a starting point and go on imagining finer horses. He's perfect. He just fills my mind. I can't imagine him made differently."

"Perhaps you can't," said the girl. "Well, Ashur would go with you if you whistled to him even."

He shook his head.

"Then I would be leaving good old Jack."

"I think good old Jack would follow you, too, Paul."

"Suppose that I had Jack and Ashur—of course I couldn't have either of them!—but just supposing—then there'd still be you left behind me!"

"I?" said Nancy in an oddly altered voice. "*That* would be hard for you, of course."

He was perfectly serious still.

"Even if I ran away," he went on, "I would have to come slipping back to try to see you. Do you know why I want school to begin? So that I can see you every day. You are *so* beautiful, Nancy!"

"Paul!" cried a breathless voice. "I don't see why you're saying this!"

He stared gloomily at the lovely waters.

"Oh, I know that you don't care! But you've started me confessing. Do you mind if I go on about you?"

"No," said she, "perhaps you'd better. You don't simply hate me for being so blunt?"

"Hate you? What an idea! Why, Nancy, sometimes I wake up in the middle of the night and I want to see you so much that

I almost jump up out of bed to go and stand under your window. Sometimes when I think of you I feel—I feel—"

He became silent.

"You were saying," she prompted in a faint voice—"when you think about me, Paul—"

"I feel the way a dog sounds when it bays the moon."

He laughed a little. Nancy did not laugh.

"I think of your mother and your father, Nancy. They have you every day!"

"And they have no other child. And I'm only a girl!"

"You?" cried Torridon. "You? Only a girl? Why, Nancy," he went on, carried away, and turning upon her, "you're the most beautiful thing in the world, and the sweetest—although you frighten me terribly, you're so cold and grave—"

He stopped in mid-gesture, mid-speech.

Great, bright, glistening tears were running rapidly down Nancy's face.

He could not believe it. But most of all it was wonderful that she did not try to conceal them. She simply kept on looking straight at him with wide eyes. As if she were looking through him, and not at him. It was like the falling of proud towers, like the rushing of great walls and the battlements to the earth, so that a city was revealed in all its undefended beauty.

"I suppose you're finished," said Nancy.

"Oh, Nancy," he stammered, "I never meant to hurt you. I never dreamed, no matter what I said, you'd ever care. Tell me what I've done, and how I can make up for it? I wouldn't care if I had to work on my knees all the rest of my life."

And he fell on his knees before her as he spoke. His heart was aching terribly. But he could not tell whether it was joy or sorrow that swelled it so greatly.

"I don't want you to work on your knees," said Nancy. "But I think you ought to kiss me, Paul!"

CHAPTER XII

★

Awakening!

They went back down the road side by side slowly, their horses close. Outstretching branches brushed at their faces. The moist odor of decaying leaves was pungent from the woods, and here and there were faintly tangle suggestions of wood smoke, drawn from far away and drooping down again, to be caught among the trees.

The day was wearing late, past the heat of the afternoon; the sun in the west was turning gold, but they rode in the shadow of the valley. All about them the autumn colors which had looked like scarlet enamel, gold leaf, and burnished Tyrian purple under the higher sun, now were filmed across with delicacy. But the heads of the trees lifted into a more brilliant beauty than ever before, yet harmonizing more, drawn from one into another by the golden softness of the light.

It was, in a way, like passing through water and looking up to the day. It was like riding through thin winter mist, except that not winter chill, but summer warmth, was above them.

As they drew down the broadening valley they looked from a gap in the trees and saw a house in the distance. All its western windows flared like polished metal; blue-white smoke rose kindly above it. And suddenly the two lovers looked at one another with inexpressible tenderness and joy.

"What shall I do?" said he. "Tell me, Nancy. You think better than I do."

"Make a small pack of your clothes to-night as soon as you

are in your room alone. Then, when the house is still, come out and to my house."

"Nancy, Nancy, what do you mean?"

"Are you frightened?"

"I'm trying not to be," he said. "I want to be a hero for you Nancy, darling."

"You will be," said she slowly, looking at him half critically, half smiling. "You always will be when the danger really comes! But you'll come?"

"If you told me to ride down into the river I'd never dream of disobeying."

They laughed together, she softly, he on a broken note.

"I'll be waiting for you before eleven o'clock," she went on. "I'll have two horses—I don't suppose that you'd bring Ashur?"

He looked down to the beautiful head of the horse and stroked the stallion's neck, and the colt turned its head and looked back to him.

"If you think it would be stealing—" said Nancy. "Well, but they'll never be able to make any use of it when you're away."

"I want him more than diamonds," he said sadly. "More than masses and masses of diamonds, Nancy dear. But I—"

He looked at her in apology, and she shrugged her shoulders.

"I'll be waiting with two horses, then. *I* don't mind stealing."

"It's all that I'd ever take from your father. And usually fathers give their children something. We'll give ours everything!"

"Oh, yes," said she, with tears in her eyes.

Then, after a little pause, she added: "By the poplars beside our house I'll wait for you. I'll have some money, too. I have some of my own."

"You give me everything, and I give you nothing," cried Torridon in anguish.

"You will give later, dear."

"I have this one thing to give you. Do you see?"

He took her hand. "Here is this ring."

"This? This is the ring of Roger Lincoln. See his initials on the seal?"

"It's all I have."

"You mustn't give this away."

"I must. I makes me happier to think of giving you something."

He slipped it on her finger. She did not look at it, but at him. There was such joy in them that for a moment they remained speechless, worshipping one another.

"We haven't decided where to go, dear."

"We'll go to the Torridons over the mountains—my people, dear Nancy."

"What would they feel if you came back to them out of death and brought a Brett with you?"

"They would love you. Everybody loves you, Nancy."

"We'd better go to a new place, Paul."

She shook her head.

"I don't care."

"We could go West. Beyond the river."

"Into the Indian countries?"

"Into the free countries," said she.

"I don't care. Oh, Nancy, what a kind world it is!"

"Now I must go home. Poor old Jack! What will he do when you're gone?"

"Would he want to come, Nancy?"

"He'd go to the end of the world with you and me."

"Shall we tell him?"

"If you want to."

"You tell him if you think best, Nancy."

"I shall, then. Good-by."

"I hate that word," said he. "Only for a little while."

She held out her arms to him and he took her close to him. There was fragrance in her hair; her eyes were looking up to him; he began to tremble.

"Paul Torridon, Paul Torridon," she said, "Heaven give you to me, and Heaven give me to you!"

He watched her ride away. When she was at the next bending of the trail she turned and waved back to him; then the trees

Coward of the Clan ☆ 71

swallowed her, but still the beat of her horse in full gallop sounded faintly.

"If that should be my last sight of her!" said Torridon to his soul.

Then he looked up and saw that the sun was down, and all the glory was stolen, even from the heads of the autumn trees. He shivered with his thought and with the sudden cold.

Then he rode home, taking the slow way, the roundabout way. It was well enough to gallop madly across country, flying the fence. But that was before he belonged to another, and now what would Nancy do without him!

Still he could not entirely believe, and before he reached the house he pinched himself once or twice, wondering if it were real, not all a dream. If, after all, she had not been making a cruel game with him, drawing out his folly so that she could tell her people, and then all of them would laugh long and loudly.

He was still tormented by that foolish dream when he came in the dusk toward the house.

It was all dark, and he wondered at that, though doubtless only in the kitchen and dining room were the lamps lit at this hour. He had no sooner come to that conclusion than three or four men started out of the brush.

"Who goes there?" cried one of them.

Paul reined in his horse. He was too shocked to make a quick answer.

"Answer!" called a voice which he thought must be that of Charlie Brett. "Answer, or we'll blow you to bits! Who are you?"

"Why, it's only Paul Torridon," said he. "Is that you, Charlie?"

"Don't 'Charlie' me, you murdering traitor!" answered young Brett. "Get off that hoss, will you? Get off and get off quick!"

Paul dismounted. He leaned against the shoulder of the stallion, unable to believe that such things could be.

Had they spied upon him and seen beautiful Nancy in his arms? That must be it!

They were all about him. Charlie caught one of his arms. Will

Brett caught another. They lashed his wrists together behind his back.

Finally he could ask: "But what does it mean, Will? What does it mean? What have I done?"

"What have you done? You ask that! You and a dozen of your sneaking Torridons ain't come down on the Harry Bretts and wiped them out, I suppose?"

"What!" breathed the boy.

"You spy!" cried Charlie, furious. "I could thrash you! I could thrash you within an inch of your life! You sneaking spy! We're gunna burn you to a crisp. Walk on!"

And they jerked Paul Torridon headlong up the path toward the house.

CHAPTER XIII

★

Down!

They dragged Torridon straight in before old John Brett, and the latter regarded him with bent brows.

"Paul Torridon," said he, "I've been keeping you in my house for twelve years or more. I've kept you in food and clothes and I've given you easy work. Your own father wouldn't've treated you half as good. How've you paid me back?"

Torridon looked earnestly back into the face of the clansman. It was not contorted with anger. It was simply hard and cold. He glanced rapidly at the others. Their passion was less under control than that of their leader. They stared at him with hungry malice.

"They say that Harry Brett has been killed," said Torridon.

"He's been raided. That was news to you, maybe?"

"It was," answered Torridon calmly.

The peril was too great to be feared. In the den of the snakes, one forgets the fear of death. So Torridon was surrounded with malice and rage.

"No," said John Brett ironically, "it's more likely that one of the Bretts themselves sent on word to those hounds of Torridons beyond the mountains! That's a pile more likely!"

Torridon was silent. He was determined not to speak until words had a chance of benefiting him.

"It was one of the Bretts," went on the leader, "that must've let the Torridons know that the three men was away from the house and that there was no one but boys and women there!"

"Did they—did they hurt—the women?" asked Paul Torridon, horror-stricken.

John Brett leaned forward in his chair.

"You didn't aim on that, eh?" said he. "You only wanted to have the men wiped out?"

"Uncle John," said Torridon earnestly, "will you tell me what I have to gain by an attack on the house of Harry Brett?"

"What has any Torridon to gain?" asked John Brett. "What have the snakes in the field to gain by sneaking up and biting a man that's sleeping?"

Torridon was silenced.

"They've come before you was ready, and I can believe that," said John Brett. "You figured that tomorrow, maybe, would be better. Then you'd slip away on Ashur. Was that the plan?"

Still Torridon did not speak, and Charles Brett stepped in from the side and struck him heavily in the face. The blow knocked him with a crash against the wall. He staggered back onto the floor, his head spinning. The hard knuckles of Charlie had split the skin over his cheek bone and a trickle of blood ran down rapidly.

Then, as his brain cleared, he looked to John Brett to hear some correction of that brutality, but there was no change in the expression of the chief.

"Answer when he speaks to you, you dog!" Charlie had said as he struck the blow.

"He's gunna play Injun on us and keep his mouth shut," suggested Will Brett.

"Shut up!" John Brett commanded his younger men. "I'll do the talking here, please. You, Torridon"—he spoke the name as though it were cinders and ashes in his mouth—"you speak up and tell me where the band of murderin' sneaks will be hiding now."

Torridon sighed.

"Is it likely that I know?" he asked.

"You dunno nothing, maybe?" asked the chief with heavy irony.

Coward of the Clan ☆ 75

"I've never spoken to a Torridon in my life—that I can remember," said the boy.

"You didn't put it into a letter?"

"I've never written to one of them, either."

"It's a lie!" broke in Charles Brett, unable to control himself. "Is it likely, I ask you now, that any skunk of a Torridon would spend twelve years without getting in touch with his people?"

John Brett accepted that suggestion with a nod of agreement.

"It ain't likely. It ain't possible," he stated. "You see, Paul, there ain't any use in trying to fool with us. It'll be easier for you to come straight out with the truth. And if you can get us to the place where we'll find your murdering crew, I'll tell you what I'll do. I'll turn you free, Paul. I'll turn you free and see you safe and livin' out of the valley! No man could offer you more than that!"

"Uncle John," said the boy in a trembling voice, "I swear—"

"My name is John Brett," corrected the patriarch sternly, "and the oaths of the Torridons never was worth the breath that was needed for the speaking of them. Talk on, and leave out the swearing."

Paul Torridon sighed again.

"I don't even know what's actually happened," said he. "And you want to kill me because I can't talk."

"You dunno?" said John Brett. "I'll tell you, then! I'll tell you that there was four boys in the house of Harry Brett. The oldest was fourteen. The youngest was nine. There was a girl of seventeen and there was Elizabeth Brett, who's forty. That house was rushed this afternoon. One of the boys got away to tell us what happened. He saw two of his brothers murdered. He saw Elizabeth Brett shot through the head—"

"Stop, stop!" whispered Torridon, and grew sick and dizzy with horror.

"You don't like it?" sneered John Brett. "There's many a cook that don't relish the dish of his own makin'! But you're gunna help to pay us back for this here, Torridon. You're going to help to pay us back!"

"Listen!" said Torridon, arguing for his life. "If the Torridons came to find some Bretts, as they came through the mountains, isn't the house of Harry Brett the first one they'd come to? Isn't that the reason that they attacked the house?"

"Then how did they know that Harry and his two brothers wasn't at the place?"

"They scouted about it, first."

"He's got an answer for everything," said Will Brett. "Ain't he a professional word-user? Ain't he a school-teacher? Let's listen to him no more! By grab, Uncle John, it's time that we tied him to a tree and built a fire under his feet—so's we could see to do our shooting!"

John Brett smiled. It was plain that the horrible suggestion was exactly after his own heart.

"You hear him, Torridon?" he asked.

"I hear him," answered the boy.

"That's what'll be done to you unless you talk up."

"There's nothing I can say."

Charlie Brett seized his shoulder viciously.

"Is that all, Uncle John?" he asked. "Can we have him?"

John Brett had lurched from his chair. The savagery of a barbarian was working in his features, and yet he controlled himself.

"Joe Brett has been taken away by the Torridons. It may be that we'll have to keep this rat to trade in for Joe. Throw him into the cellar. And keep a watch at the cellar door. Tie him hand and foot and keep a watch. If he gets away I'll skin you and hang up your hides to show the Bretts what happens to fools!"

They carried poor Torridon away with them, wrenching and dragging him along.

The creaking cellar door was heaved open and big Charlie said: "Lemme put him down there. Tie his legs with that rope, Will!"

It was done. The legs of Torridon were lashed securely together.

"Now stand him up!" directed Charles Brett.

Coward of the Clan ☆ 77

They stood up Torridon like a nine-pin. And Charlie Brett drove at him with all his might.

Excess of malice spoiled his aim. Instead of landing full in the center of the face, the blow glanced on the side of Torridon's head, but nevertheless it was enough to hurl him backwards down the steps.

He felt himself going and purposely made his limbs and body limp. He landed at the bottom of the steps on the damp floor, rolled over and over, and crashed against a big box.

There he lay.

He was too overwhelmed with woe to think clearly, but he was able to say to himself that after bright day comes the black night.

Now Nancy was at her house. She, too, was hearing the tale of the raid upon the house of Harry Brett. Would she believe that he had conspired against the slaughtered family?

Then he tried to work out the matter in his mind—tried to conceive how people who bore his name, in whose veins his blood flowed, could have contemplated such a horrible massacre—far less, actually have done the thing.

And after that he lay still without even a thought. He heard feet stamp on the floor above him. He heard loud voices, once or twice. Faintly he could hear the murmur of ordinary conversation. And after a long time there was a rattle of hoofs.

The first division of hunters for the marauding Torridons were coming back, no doubt! And what sort of a report would they make? Had they found their quarry? Had they shot them down like dogs? Or were the destroyers safely away through the woods and into the throat of the mountain pass?

No one came near him for several hours. Then the cellar door was lifted and a glimmer of lantern light broke into the pitchy darkness.

Charles Brett, with old Aunt Ellen behind him, came down into the improvised dungeon. He kicked the prisoner roughly in the side.

"Wake up," he commanded, though he could see by his lantern that the eyes of the boy were wide open.

"Leave him be," said Aunt Ellen. "Leave him be. I'm gunna just sit down here and comfort him a little. You go on up and leave the lantern down here with me."

Charlie merely paused to leer at Torridon.

"Things has changed a little, eh?" said he. "You ain't so much the cock of the walk now. I'll show you who's on top, you hound!"

He left them, and Aunt Ellen sat down on a broken box beside the boy and uncovered a steaming dish.

"You gotta eat, dear Paul," said she. "You gotta eat and save your strength, because maybe you'll be needing all of it one of these days!"

CHAPTER XIV

★

The Tale Of Torridon

It was a good roast beef, cut in large chunks. And Torridon, wriggling until he could prop his back against a musty barrel's side, ate heartily and then drank the coffee which she had brought with her also.

She looked like a witch, crouched over an evil deed. But as he ate she patted him. She brushed the mold and the damp of the cellar from his face and hair. Then she smiled and nodded at him.

"Aunt Ellen," he could not help bursting out, "I always thought that you hated me, and here you are taking care of me! The only one who cares at all!"

"It's little that I can do for you, lad," said she.

"You can go to Uncle John and tell him that I've sworn to you that I never was in touch with the Torridons. And Heaven knows if I had been there I would have fought to keep the poor children safe from those brutes! Aunt Ellen, it's not possible that he or you believe that I could have helped at such a thing!"

"I wouldn't dare go near to Uncle John this night," said the crone. "He's as black as the raven and as cold as steel, since the boys come home and said that they couldn't get no trace of the killers."

"No trace!" murmured the prisoner.

"It's a weary, weary night," said Aunt Ellen. "There ain't been the like of it in the mountains since the night when Hugh Torridon and his people was killed!"

"Who was Hugh Torridon?" asked the boy.

"Now, now, now!" said she. "Would you be wantin' me to believe that you never heard tell of Hugh Torridon?"

"Never," he assured her earnestly.

"Ah, but that's a story!" said she. "And if I stay here to tell it to you—"

"Do stay, Aunt Ellen," he pleaded. "Do stay, because after you go I'll have all the long, black, cold night ahead of me. I'll be half dead before morning with the damp and the chill, and the horrible smell of the rats, Aunt Ellen!"

"Will you, now?" said she, running her hand gently over his head again. "But what if I stay so long down her comfortin' you that John Brett raises his voice after me? He's got a voice that has to be heard!"

She did not wait for an answer, but went on: "Hugh Torridon! Hugh Torridon! And you never heard of him?"

"I always was afraid to ask about the Torridons," said the boy. "It always made the Bretts angry to be reminded that there were more people of my name in the world."

"D'you know why there's any Torridons alive to-day?" she asked curiously.

"Tell me, Aunt Ellen."

"Because of Hugh Torridon. It was him that brought the Torridons up from nothing. They was beaten. Their backs was against the wall when I was a girl. They didn't have nothing. They was so poor you wouldn't believe it. And then Hugh come.

"He was young, but he could talk. He persuaded the whole pack of them to move across the mountains and start farming there. The climate was better and the ground was richer, and pretty soon the Torridons on that side of the mountains was a lot better off than ever they had been on this side. It was a surprisin' thing how quick they began to make money and get respectable lookin' again! Pretty soon they was about as rich as the Bretts!"

She paused and waggled her head at this important thought.

Then she went on: "After they was strong enough, with all good horses and with all the best kind of pistols and rifles and knives, and everything that men kill deer and each other with, they begun to march in back through the mountains, and when they found a Brett here and there, they just nacherally shot him.

"Hugh Torridon had the leading of them. He was an iron

man. Bullets would bounce off of him, the young men here used to say. Uncle John was a young man, then!"

She chuckled with the idea.

"The Torridons, they kept walking deeper and deeper into our valleys. I remember when they swept all the cattle off my pa's place."

Then she went on: "This man died, and he left a young son, also called Hugh; and the young son, he was raised to remember how his father died and to try to get even for it."

"And how *did* the first Hugh Torridon die, Aunt Ellen?"

"As he was ridin' down the river side," said she. "There was a couple of clever young Bretts lyin' in the brush, and they shot him after he'd gone by."

"Through the back!" said the boy, writhing.

"One bullet was under the shoulder blade and another was right in the middle of the spine. He didn't make no noise. He just died and dropped out of the saddle.

"Now then, his son, the second Hugh, he come up to his manhood as big and as brave as his father, but he didn't have the brain. Brains is what wins for everybody. You got brains, poor Paul! That's why you been amounting to something. But anyways, I gotta tell you that this second Hugh, he couldn't have no pleasure in staying on the far side of the mountains, and so he built him a house of strong logs right over our heads on this slope. We always could see the smoke going up from his place. And he done a lot of harm to us, until finally Uncle John thought it would be a good idea to make a truce. So a truce was made between the Torridons and the Bretts.

"And after that a couple of years went by, peaceful and quiet, but all the while Uncle John was plannin' and waitin'. And finally he went down with ten good men. Only ten, because more might've made too much noise. He took those men and went to the house of Hugh Torridon and he pried the front door off its hinges, very quiet.

" 'Who's there?' " sings Hugh Torridon from the darkness.

"But already they was inside. They got into the first room where there was Hugh Torridon's wife and baby. And Hugh Torridon, when he heard them two screaming—he sort of lost his wits!"

"Don't! Don't!" cried the boy. "You don't mean that they murdered a woman with a baby beside her?"

"A Torridon is a Torridon, young or old, male or female. Uncle John is the one who knows that! But I was tellin' you that Hugh Torridon come smashing along down the hall and got at that room, where there was two of his family dead, and where there was ten armed men waiting for him; and when he come along the ten got a little mite afraid, because he was so brave. They locked and bolted the door of that room, and then they waited, and Hugh Torridon busted down that door the way a bull would bust down a pasture gate.

"He come in and they let off all their rifles, and they shot Torridon with six bullets through the body and the legs. But he went on and got hold on one of them, and that was Jim Brett, and he strangled Jim Brett as he died."

"What a glorious man he must have been!" cried the boy.

"He was a great Torridon," nodding, she agreed, "only that he didn't have the brains of his pa. But after he'd killed Jim the rest of the Bretts got a little mite angry, and they went through the house and they killed every one. There was only one boy left that had been knocked on the head and fell like dead.

"When they had cooled off a little and counted the eight dead bodies, then they begun to think of starting home, and just then the boy that had seemed to be senseless, he got up on his feet and began staggering around.

"They'd cooled off, as I was sayin', so that they didn't have the heart to finish him. They just let him live, and Uncle John, he had a pretty good idea, because he said: 'I'll take him home and raise him up, and we'll make a man of him, in Jim's place!' "

She paused.

"Took him home!" echoed poor Torridon. "Took him here! Aunt Ellen have you been telling me the story of my grandfather, and my father and mother?"

"I have!" she said. She added: "And your baby brother, and your two sisters, and your cousin who—"

Coward of the Clan ☆ 83

"Don't!" whispered the boy. "It hurts me terribly! Ah, Aunt Ellen, but I had to know!"

"Of course you did, honey!"

She raised the lantern so that it shone into the eyes of the captive, but in so doing, she allowed it to fall, unawares, upon her own eyes, and Torridon was amazed to see that she was grinning with toothless, wicked malice.

Then he could understand! It was all a device of her ancient hatred. She had wanted to sit by his side and watch him while she opened wounds of which he never had dreamed. This was her fiendish pleasure, and now she stood up.

"I dunno what else I can do for you, sonny. My stories don't seem to rest you none."

"Only leave me!" said he.

"Then lie and think," said she, thrusting her wicked face closer to his. "You lie and think about the good day that's comin' before you, and you eat plenty of good meat and keep yourself fat and strong, because you'll need all of your strength when they take you out and tie you to a tree, my son!"

She turned from him, shuffling away with the lantern. It cast vast shadows that swung up against the ceiling and then down and out before her. It made the room seem awash.

Then she was gone, and the cellar door was closed with a heavy, smashing sound.

The ears of the captive must have been attuned by sorrow, for he could hear the voice of Will Brett saying calmly: "You spent a long time down there!"

"My business couldn't be done quick," she replied. "Gimme your arm into the house, Billy dear!"

After that the long silence began once more and ran on into the morning. Yet Paul did not grow irritated by the blank time. His thoughts ran before him like a rapidly flowing river. He was seeing all the past of his race. Before that the name of Torridon had had no content to him. The malice of Aunt Ellen with her recital of horrors had given him a history and his people a past. He was almost grateful to her for the torture of that story.

CHAPTER XV

★

A Soft Voice Calls

Ten days of blackness, utter blackness, passed.

He was fed once a day. He was shifted into a corner room of the cellar. There it was damper, wetter. Twice during the ten days heavy rains came, and the water covered the floor on which he lay.

He wondered profoundly why he did not sicken and die. But he had not so much as a cold in the head. It was not disease that troubled him. It was the constant misery of the wet, the dirt, the darkness, the scampering of rats, which repeatedly crossed his hands and face. And once, stretching out his hand at a noise, he passed his fingers along the sliding back of a snake.

So ten days passed.

Then he was visited by John Brett in person. The old leader threw the door back and came heavily down the stairs. He pushed his lantern into the face of the captive and leaned above him.

"Are you awake?"

"I'm awake," said the boy.

"I've brought news for you."

"Yes?" he answered calmly, for he had given up hope.

"We offered you in exchange for Joe. But they say they don't believe that we've got a real Torridon. No real Torridon would've lived twelve years with the Bretts."

He paused to allow this information to sink in.

"They won't give up Joe Brett for you," he concluded. "So you see what they done for you? We gotta kill you, my boy.

Coward of the Clan ☆ 85

Duty to do it. Only it's night, now. We gotta wait for the morning to have light to see the show. So long, Paul! I hope you keep your head up high in the mornin', the way that a Torridon should!"

He turned away. At the door he paused and threw over his shoulder: "She's been here beggin' for you, draggin' herself at my knees, weepin' and cryin' for you. But though you might be able to make a fool out of the Brett women, you ain't gunna make a fool out of me through their talk!"

He slammed the door, turned the key with a screech in the rusty bolt, and then stamped away.

Paul Torridon was almost glad that waiting was over. It was not death, but the manner of it that was terrible. But at least he could depend on good old Jack. Jack Brett would never see him suffer, but would drive a bullet cheerfully through his heart, and so the merciful end!

The wind came up. He heard its distant whining and moaning. And the rain drove against the house in rattling gusts. By fits and starts, the squalls of that storm rushed against the house, and Torridon was glad of the storm, too, because it would help to fill the long hours of the night. He hoped that it would rave and scream in the morning, too, when he was led out to die. For he had only that one grim hope left—that he might find the strength to die with a smile on his lips, as a brave man should. He even hoped that, before the end, he could be able to find a speech of sharp defiance, and taunting, so that the memory of how he had died might have a noble place in the mind of Nancy, since that was all that he could leave to her!

A leak had sprung somewhere in the very center of the cellar. A quick, sharp rattling fall seemed to come at his very door. The wind howled far off; another gust of rain smashed on the house and again he could hear that clatter at his door.

And then, was it not the faint, harsh murmur of the hinges, slowly turned?

He braced himself. There was such a thing as a midnight murder to defeat the hand of justice, which was beginning to be extended more and more often into this region where the gun had been the only judge.

Then a soft voice called: "Paul Torridon!" A man's voice; quiet, pitched just with the fall of the rain.

He said loudly: "Here I am! If you've come to murder me, strike a light. I want to see your face."

Something crouched beside him. His body turned to rigid steel.

"Torridon, I'm Roger Lincoln!"

That name dissolved the world and left the blackness and the cold and the dark of despair far off, and brought the prisoner suddenly into the light of warm hope and comfort.

Roger Lincoln!

The ropes were cut away from his hands, from his feet. He tried to rise, but Lincoln thrust him back again. There was wonderful power in the famous hand of that hero.

"Lie still. Close your eyes. Breathe deeply, and relax!"

He obeyed those quick orders with perfect attention.

And then the strong hands began to move, rubbing his numbed muscles, bringing sense and power into his nerves, into his whole body. Paul began to tingle, where the ropes had long worn at the flesh, until the tingling made him almost cry out.

"Now," said Roger Lincoln, ceasing from his labor. "Now, try your feet."

Paul stood up in the dark.

He found himself ridiculously weak. His head went round. He would have fallen, but the other clutched and steadied him.

"This is bad," he heard Lincoln mutter. "This is very bad!"

He paused, breathing hard from the work of that rubbing. Then he said: "I've brought an extra pistol. Can you use a pistol at all?"

"Yes."

"Here it is. Double-barreled. It shoots straight and it's not too heavy. Never fire till I give the word, and I won't give the word unless it's the last chance. And—"

"Hush!" said Paul Torridon.

He had lain those endless hours in the place until his ear could make out everything, everywhere in the cellar.

Some one had raised the cellar door; the big, flat, massive door.

Outside that was always at least one guard. John Brett took no chances.

"How did you come in?" whispered Paul.

"Through the door," said Roger Lincoln. "The hail knocked them silly a little while ago. Then I went in when they hunted cover. They're tired of their work."

"They know that you're here!" said Torridon in an agony of conviction.

"How can they?"

"They're opening the cellar door now."

"Follow me; straight behind me, if you can."

"I can, I think. If you go slowly, slowly!"

He concentrated. He fought his reeling head, his clumsy, weak limbs, and made them go straight. So he marched ahead. They were through the door of the cell which had held him, and then a suddenly unhooded lantern flamed against their eyes. And behind lantern light they saw the dim silhouettes of four men, guns in hand.

CHAPTER XVI

★

On To The West!

Long afterward, when he thought of that moment, Torridon went cold with fear and horror; but at the moment, overriding all else, was the knowledge that he had only two bullets in that double-barreled pistol, that he had nothing wherewith to load again, and that each of those two bullets must bring down a man.

At the gleam of the lantern he had stumbled and fallen flat as its rays swept over them. Roger Lincoln had leaped to the side with catlike suddenness. And three guns boomed and flashed from the hands of the Bretts—three rapid, long flashes which lighted up the dark of the cellar.

At the left-hand and last flash, Torridon fired his right barrel. And he heard the slump of a body to the floor. He had fired just beneath the flash—his bullet should have found the body; perhaps the heart.

He remembered, afterward, how he had thought out those details. Roger Lincoln had fired two shots to his right.

Then a vague form loomed above Torridon and hurled itself at him with a sound like the growl of an infuriated dog. Up at the head of the lunging shadow he fired. A heavy weight struck him, rolled loosely off. And he got to his hands and knees just as Roger Lincoln leaned above him.

"Are you hurt?"

"Not hurt, Roger!"

"Thank goodness!"

To make speed, Roger Lincoln caught up the youngster and heaved him over one shoulder. He rushed up the steps, with a

Coward of the Clan ☆ 89

sound of stifled groaning following him from the cellar. Two shots followed them. One bullet landed with a soft thud. Torridon was sure that it must have struck the flesh of his rescuer, but Roger Lincoln went on, unhesitating.

The door of the cellar was cast wide.

Out from the house rushed half a dozen forms, armed, shouting with excitement.

"What's happening? Who's there? Stop those two men!" shouted the voice of John Brett. "Where's a lantern?"

There was no lantern. Through the dusk, Torridon thought they might escape, but Roger Lincoln did not attempt to avoid the group. Instead, he strode on straight toward them, straight through them.

"It's Roger Lincoln!" he called. "He's down there with Torridon. He's broken into the place—he's killed Charlie, I think. And we downed one of 'em—"

"Roger Lincoln!" cried John Brett.

And all of them rushed like bulldogs toward the point of danger. Several others swarmed down from the house. The door was swinging and crashing.

Then they turned the corner, and Roger Lincoln lowered Torridon to the ground.

"Are you hurt?" he asked.

"No," said Torridon.

"Come on with me then. My horse is near here."

They began to run, and no sooner did the strain of the muscles begin that Torridon felt a long, burning pain that went through his body and up his side.

"The gray can carry you—I'll run alongside," said Roger Lincoln. "I started with a second horse; it went dead lame. I couldn't wait till to-morrow—"

"I would have been dead to-morrow," gasped Torridon.

They broke through a group of trees.

"I'll get Ashur!"

"Aye, if we could get him!"

"They're after us!" cried Lincoln.

A wave of angry shouting broke upward from the cellar door and spread abroad into the night.

"I'm going to take the gray mare," said Roger Lincoln. "I'll ride across them and get them after me if I can. You go on to the barn and get Ashur. Do you want to try that?"

"I'll try that!"

They had reached the covert in which Comanche was hidden, and now Roger Lincoln flashed away on her; and Torridon ran for his life toward the stable.

He could feel the wound throbbing down his side now. It sent electric thrills of fear through him. What would happen to him? How far would his life last?

He climbed the last fence. He was through the rear stable door and Ashur's whinny of greeting met him in the dark. And here was Ashur, plunging, snorting with joy, like a dog long separated from a loved master.

In all his life, Ashur never had failed to see young Torridon every day. Now he was frantic with pleasure. And nothing Torridon called in the way of softly muttered orders had any effect on him.

He pitched off the saddle when it was dragged onto his back. Only when the bridle and bit had been given to him did he quiet, and then, from the distance, Torridon heard voices.

And there was left to him only Ashur, and an unloaded pistol.

Frantically he caught up the saddle and dragged it over the back of the stallion again. The cinches swung readily into his hand, and he jerked them home on the buckles.

"Who's there?" some one was calling. Lantern light began to turn the stall posts into a myriad tall shadows, pitching to and fro like waves before a gale.

"It's some one at Ashur! Quick, it may be him!"

Clearly, clearly rang that voice, freezing the heart of Torridon. No Brett could miss a target fairly seen. Only the night, which had covered him before, might cover him now!

He climbed into the saddle. He had a certain nervous force in his hands. With that, he dragged his trembling, failing body. The light was rushing down upon him, like a ship driving through a sea. There were more than two. Three men were coming, and may Heaven defend him!

He twisted Ashur from the stall. The stallion heard his whisper. Like a human being, aware of danger, it slipped forward with stealthy steps, and the rear door of the stable was just before them, swinging half shut in the wind.

And then the full tide of the lantern light washed over them.

"There he is!"

"Shoot!"

"Shoot for the horse! Anything to get him!"

Then Paul called: "Ashur!"

And Ashur leaped for the half-shut door, with Torridon bending along his neck. It was too narrow a space for horse and man to go through, but Ashur turned his head and, like a man, gave the door his shoulder—gave it such a blow that it crashed open under the shock.

Three guns filled the barn with thunder. Horses, frightened, began to neigh and stamp, and Torridon was out under the wet skies. Noise everywhere, from the house, from the stable!

Had the stallion been struck?

There was no way to tell at once. His great heart would not fail until his blood ran out. And he would tell time like an hourglass to the last running of the sand.

Torridon turned the black toward the road. Three fences, big, black, shaggy with the night, rose before them. Strangely large they loomed, but Ashur went over them softly, lightly. Surely he was not struck! But what if he were laying down his life for his master? Was the life of any man worth such a price?

They gained the road before the house. Other horsemen were pouring out from the door of the barn behind him. But there, glimmering through the dark before him, he saw a horseman— Roger Lincoln on his gray?

He shouted, and the ringing voice of Roger Lincoln struck back to him. Then he was with that hero from the plains! And the pursuit was beating behind them.

Let them come! Let them ride the hearts out of their horses; they would no more catch this pair than they would catch the eagles in the air with their bare hands!

Swiftly they slid away. Like quicksilver flowed the mare. Like the wind ran the black. For a blinding mile they ran, and then the silver mare slipped behind. A neck back, a length back!

"Steady!" called Roger Lincoln. "You'll fly away from me, lad!"

Torridon drew in the stallion. They ran more easily, with long bounds that devoured the distance. There was not even a sound of pursuit, now, behind them.

At moonrise they stopped.

Then they looked to the horses. Ashur was untouched.

"And you?" said Roger Lincoln.

"I'm scratched along the side, I think."

It was only a scratch, a glancing cut which might have taken his life, if it had been a fraction of an inch deeper.

Lincoln bound it up.

"Now what?" he asked.

"I must go to the right, down the next road. I—I have to see a girl, if I can, before I ride on, Roger."

"That's pretty Nancy?"

"Do you know about her?"

"Every one knows about her and you. Jack told me."

"Jack?"

"She gave Jack my ring that you'd given her. It was Jack that found me and sent me back."

"Bless him! But—"

"She's not in her father's house. She's been sent away to the West—to the house of a cousin."

"Then West, West!" said Torridon feverishly. "How far will it be?"

"Ten days of careful riding," said Roger Lincoln. "Into a new world, lad."

"And can we find her?" Torridon persisted.

"Of course we can find her," came the great man's answer.

"West, then," said Torridon, "if you'll take me.'

"Look to Ashur," said the plainsman. "Will he fail you?"

"Never."

"He is only a horse," said Roger Lincoln, "and I'll hope to show you that I'm a man, Torridon!"

PART TWO
★
The Man from the Sky

CHAPTER XVII

★

Alone

When Torridon wakened, the sun was not five minutes below the horizon, and he jumped from his blankets and reproached himself in silent gloom. For many days, now, he had been striving to imitate the habits of Roger Lincoln. That great hunter had observed that life on the plains was best begun with the first grayness of dawn, and best ended with the total dark. Or, he would say, a little more morning, a little more evening, made one day into two. Even the Indians might be gained upon in this manner, and as for the ordinary whites who trekked across the plains, they worked like moles, a step at a time, blindly.

But here was another day stolen almost upon Torridon before he was on his feet.

He was surprised that the fire was not burning; but as a matter of fact, Roger Lincoln was nowhere around. The gray mare grazed close to the camp, near tall Ashur. But Roger Lincoln apparently had gone off to hunt; his rifle was missing with him.

This was not extraordinary. Between the dark and the dawn always was the best hunting, he used to observe; when the plains animals were least aware of the world, their senses yet unsharpened, and before they were aware that the sheltering blanket of the night had been withdrawn from them they might be stolen upon and dispatched.

The sun had a dazzling eye out over the plain before Torridon had finished these observations. In a moment more he was above the edge of the sky. It was time to prepare breakfast. As a matter of fact, Roger Lincoln did not like to make fires in the day; the thin arms of smoke which rose waved signals to a great distance and attracted unknown eyes.

"Everything you don't know is dangerous," Lincoln was apt to say.

Therefore, in the preparation of the fire, Torridon was extra careful. In a small patch of brush near by he found some dead branches, and these he broke up small, and lighted and maintained the smallest of fires. He had learned from Lincoln, too, that a great flare of fire is not necessary for cookery. A small tongue of flame playing constantly right on the bottom of a pan will accomplish great results. And it is a fine art to gradually extend a bed of coals which casts off no smoke at all.

By great efforts and perfect concentration, he was assured when he had breakfast prepared that there had not been more than one or two puffs of smoke large enough to be worth noticing. The rest was a fume that hardly could have been visible two hundred yards away.

When he had finished the cookery he sat down to wait. It might be that Lincoln had found an attractive shot, wounded the game, and been drawn far afield to track it.

So he waited a full hour, ate a cold meal, and settled himself again.

The sun was high, moving slowly through the heavens, and the heat became momently greater. The air was delicate with the scent of the May bloom of the prairie. And he began to drowse.

Since they began their long march for Fort Kendry, and had voyaged beyond the settlements into the emptiness of the plains, Lincoln had insisted on hard journeys every day, and Torridon, in consequence, had been put through a severe grilling. He had grown thinner and more brown in the open air. His muscles were taking on a tough fiber such as they never had possessed before, but nevertheless it had often been torture. He was just beginning to be inured to the labor and the constant racking in the saddle. If it had not been for the silken gaits of the great black stallion he knew that he never could have kept up his end. But now he saw a chance to rest.

Roger Lincoln, no doubt, never would have dreamed of drowsing in the uncovered nakedness of the prairie during the day, but that was because he was almost more panther than man. And young Torridon felt that he was gathered into a deep security by the very fact that, no matter what enemy the prairie might hold, it also held Roger Lincoln. To the wisdom, the skill, the courage of that famous man he implicitly bowed.

So he fell sound asleep, with his head in the shadow of a small bush. There would be a quiet lecture from Lincoln when that hunter returned to the camp, but the joy of relaxing in the sun which drew the soreness from his muscles was more than the youngster could forego.

He wakened at last with a start, feeling that he had been hearing whispering voices. His heart was beating wildly, and he got to his knees and looked cautiously about him.

Lincoln's gray mare and Ashur still were grazing near by; nothing stirred on the plain except the shining foot-prints of the wind upon the grass, now and again.

He was reassured by this sense of peace until, glancing down, he saw that his shadow lay small at his feet. The sun was straight overhead, and he had slept away the entire morning. Half a day had gone by, and there was no trace of Roger Lincoln's return!

In seven hours he could have gone afoot nearly twenty miles out and twenty miles back. But it might be that, starting back with a heavy load of newly shot game, he had stepped in a hole and wrenched an ankle. Even Roger Lincoln could not be entirely impervious to accident!

Torridon made up two packs, carefully, like a schoolboy working to please a master, for Lincoln was shrewd and keen critic of everything that his pupil did. He knew how to make silence thunder with his displeasure.

When that work seemed fairly well done, then he mounted Ashur, and taking the gray on the lead, he began to ride through the prairie. Lincoln had showed him how to go about such a thing, using a starting point as the center of widening circles, and so tracing a larger and larger web, observing every inch of the ground.

For two hours he kept Ashur in brisk motion. At the end of that time he paused at the verge of a river bed and began to arrange his thoughts. There had been no sight and there had been no sign of his companion. Through, from the back of a horse, half a dozen times he had been on low hillocks from which the plain was visible for many miles around, nothing had moved into his ken.

He freshened his grip on the heavy rifle which he had learned to balance across the pommel of his saddle, and fought back the panic which leaped up in his breast. Something had happened to Roger Lincoln. He swallowed hard when he thought what that meant.

Fort Kendry, where he hoped to find Nancy Brett, still was eight days' march away from them, Lincoln had said, and as for its direction, he had only the slightest idea. He could see, now, that he had been following the great scout with half of his brain asleep, trusting blindly to the guidance of his companion and never trying to think out the trail problems for himself.

He was lost, then. He was totally lost!

Across his mind went grim memories of tales he had heard from Lincoln about the plains—men who wandered for weary weeks, with no game in sight, with no glimpse of a human being, until chance saved them—saved one out of a hundred who passed through such a time.

And he, Paul Torridon, ignorant totally of all that a lonely man should do, ignorant of the way to return, ignorant of the trail which lay ahead, what would become of him?

Dreadful panic gripped him, shook him. He was lost!

He got down off his horse and took out paper and pencil. He wrote swiftly:

> To whoever finds my body. If my gun and my horse are near, you are welcome to them. Treat the horse well. It is the best I ever have seen. Only—if you wish to ride him, don't wear spurs. They drive him mad. Whatever I have you are welcome to.
>
> But for Heavens' sake take the inclosed note to Nancy

Brett, at Fort Kendry. She is living there with her cousin, Samuel Brett, and his wife.

He signed that "Paul Torridon," and then he went on to write, more slowly:

> DEAR NANCY: I write this knowing that I am hopelessly lost on the plains and that I haven't one chance in a hundred of coming out alive. This will reach you only if white men and not red find my body.
>
> Dear Nancy, you will have heard terrible things about the way we broke out from John Brett's house. They kept me locked in the cellar for ten days. They did what they could to torment me, and on the eleventh morning they were to finish me off. That night Roger Lincoln came. He managed to slip past the guards and get to me. They surprised us as we were trying to get out. In the fight, I know that we shot down four men. I hope that all of them lived; if not, I want you to know that we only fired because we were fighting for our lives.
>
> Then Roger Lincoln started to take me west to Fort Kendry, because he had heard from Jack that you were to be taken there. We got to this point; then Roger disappeared one morning from the camp.
>
> Whether some animal killed him, or Indians surprised him, I don't know. I only know that he didn't come back. If he is dead, Heaven be good to him. He was the bravest and the best man in the world!
>
> Oh, Nancy, if I had known that our ride down the valley was to be the last time that I should ever see you, I never would have left. But that chance is gone. I'd think that my life was thrown away—because I've never done anything worth living for—but I know that for one day, at least, you loved me, dearest Nan, and that is more than the world to me. And when I think of you now, it makes my heart ache more than death can do!
>
> Beautiful, beautiful Nan, good-by. Remember me.   PAUL

When he had written this he put it away in his wallet, and then he gave himself up to sad thoughts until tears came into his eyes, and even trickled down his cheeks.

Something stirred on the inner side of the river bank. He caught up his rifle from the ground beside him and listened, hair on end. It was as stealthy rustling, a stealing noise, which seemed to his straining senses to come straight toward him.

And then, above the bank, came the proud head of a stag; and a beautiful young deer stood outlined against the sky just above him.

CHAPTER XVIII

★

Which Way Now?

His heartbreaking sorrow he forgot with desperate speed. Here was food for a month, if only he could catch it!

At the leap of his rifle to his shoulder, the deer saw him and leaped not back, but straight ahead. It was a blurred streak at which he fired. The racing animal gave three tremendous bounds, the last high in the air, and fell dead.

Torridon stood up and looked to the white-hot sky in mute thankfulness. Certainly this was a gift from heaven to him, the novice hunter!

Feverishly, paying no heed to the future, but all for the sake of the future, he worked during the rest of that day. He had been shown by Lincoln the proper way to strip off a pelt, but he rather hacked the good hide away. The meat was what he wanted, and that meat he cut into long strips. Out of the willows along the river bed he prepared many slender sticks, and these he used to hang the venison upon.

How long would the sun take to dry the meat thoroughly?

Then night came on him as his labors neared an end. He was tired with excitement and with work. He lay down and slept like a child.

Once, before morning, Ashur neighed softly, and stamped. Torridon was on his feet at once, and found the great black stallion beside him, almost trampling on him, while the pricked ears and the glistening eyes of the horse were turned toward the north. Yonder in the darkness some danger was moving—coyote, wolf, bear, Indian, renegade white! He knew that the two fine horses would be enough to enlarge the heart of any trapper with fierce greed, and as for the Indians, Roger Lincoln had assured him that any Indian on the plains would pay all but life for the possession even of the famous gray mare, to say nothing of that matchless king of runners, Ashur.

Still lay Torridon, one ear close to the ground, as Ashur veered a little, and pointed now more to the east. Yet Torridon heard nothing whatever. A long half hour—and then Ashur put down his head and began to graze once more. The danger had ended!

And Torridon, though he told himself that he could not sleep again after such a shock, was almost instantly in slumber once more. After all, there was Ashur, more keenly alive and alert, more dependable than any human sentinel.

The morning was only past him while his brain still was befogged. His first thought was: I have lived one day in the desert, and the finish of me is not yet! No, there's the meat that will keep me alive for a long time if I use patience!

It was a day of burning heat. It ate through the coat of Torridon, stout homespun though it was, and fairly singed his shoulders. It covered the prairie with shimmering lines of heat as with a veil, and it wrought wonders upon the meat, as though a slow fire were playing on the wet venison.

All that day and the next Torridon watched the curing of the meat. But by that time he began to feel that the prairie, after all, was not so totally dangerous. Running down the edge of the narrow rivulet which wound back and forth through the pebbles and the boulders of the stream bottom, there seemed to be a constant procession of rabbits. He did not need to shoot them. The simplest little traps, constructed as Lincoln had showed him how to do, were sufficient to snare the jacks. Torridon lived well and watched his venison cure to strips withered and black looking, hard as boards, but promising much nutriment. He had a pack of that food prepared presently, and then he asked himself where he should go.

What would Roger Lincoln do if he were not dead and ever managed to escape from the troubles which now held him? It seemed obvious to Torridon. In the first place, the hunter would inquire at Fort Kendry to learn if the traveler had come. In the second place, Lincoln would go to the spot of that last camp and there strive to take up the trail.

So Torridon went back, and where the fire had been built, he drove down a strong stake. The stake he split, and in the split he fixed firmly a bit of paper which simply said:

> DEAR ROGER: I've decided to go south to the first river, and then follow that river toward the right—west. I'll keep on it to its source. I don't know what else to do, and I'd go mad if I stayed here in the loneliness without a move of some kind.
>
> PAUL TORRIDON.

There was nothing else that he could think of to say. He added as a post-script:

> If I turn to the left from the river, I'll put two blazes on a big tree. If I turn to the right, I'll put one.

That might, eventually, be the means for bringing Roger Lincoln to the trail of him.

Then he went back to the river to the south, by the banks of which he had killed the deer and cured its venison. He turned to the right and journeyed slowly up its banks.

He had no reason to journey fast; rather he dreaded leaving the stream by coming to the end of it. For a day he went up it, and then came to a fork. A mere trickle of water descended each big gorge. Apparently later in the summer the bed would be entirely dry, and only in the winter the water roared down in floods.

He hesitated for a long time at that division of the trail. Both forks seemed of an equal size. Neither carried more water than the other, and as for their direction, one pointed a little northwest, the other a little south of west. There was not a whit to choose between them.

He chose the northern one, therefore, because this made it unnecessary for him to cross either of the beds of the streams.

Up the northern fork he continued for two days, and all that time he had no cause to use up his precious stock of dried venison. Rabbit meat was plentiful, and rabbit was not yet a weary diet to him.

The third day he found the stream diminishing rapidly in size. And before noon he came to another forking. Once more he paused to consider his course.

At the junction of the two streams high water had carved off the point of land and left there a little triangular island, with one or two trees supported on it, a willow, and an oak, half of whose roots had been washed bare, so that the trunk sagged perceptibly to the north and seemed in danger of being carried away in the floods of the next winter.

The northern branch of the stream here swung off sharply to the right; the southern branch pointed almost due west, and this was the one which he determined to take as his guide in these blind wanderings. So he rode down the steep bank of the gulley and crossed both streams above the fork.

He regarded the upstream face of the island with curiosity. It was cracked across and written upon with long indentations. The soil of which it was composed seemed falling slowly apart and waiting for only one more thrust of winter to tumble it into a complete ruin.

Drawn by his curiosity, he climbed to the top of the bank and there he clutched his rifle to his shoulder. For he saw a man dressed in the full regalia of an Indian of the warpath stretched on his side beneath the shadow of the two trees. Beside him stood a water bottle, a bow, and a sheath of arrows. His head was pillowed on a small bank of earth, apparently heaped up by him to serve for that particular purpose.

Torridon moved nearer, paused, and again examined the prostrate man with care.

There was no movement, he thought at first, and he had come to the determination that the fellow must be dead, when, observing narrowly, it seemed to Torridon that the elbow of the

Coward of the Clan ☆ 105

man moved a little. He looked again, and made sure that the Indian was only sleeping, and that the elbow was raised or lowered a trifle by his breathing.

Through this time he heard from behind him, to the north and west, a rumbling as of thunder, but thunder in the great distance, and now it seemed to Torridon that he was afraid to look behind him, as though friends of this sleeper were rushing upon him with many horses, ready to overwhelm him. This thunder was the beating of the hoofs.

It was a foolish fancy. But in the meantime, Torridon did not know what to do. A man armed and well dressed could not be in any great need, though it appeared that this warrior was extremely pinched of face—which might have been a mere characteristic of an unhealthy Indian. However, he was a native of the plains, and therefore he safely could be left to them.

Torridon gave up all thought of waking the sleeper or of offering him any succor. What concerned him was only to retreat as softly as possible by the way in which he had come. Yet a silent retreat would not be easy. There were sticks and stones which might stir under his foot. Once wakened, the Indian would be sure to look about for the cause of the disturbance, and Torridon, perhaps halfway down the bank, would receive a bullet in the back.

Then what could he do?

He had two horses to manage, now left in the little gorge, and sure to make noise as they went on over the stones and pebbles.

There was only one safe alternative, and that was to shoot the sleeper. It seemed to Torridon that, had Roger Lincoln been in a similar position he simply would have roused the fellow with a call, allowed him to arm himself, and then have put a bullet through his brain.

That was Roger Lincoln, the invincible warrior. But what of himself, the novice of the plains?

He bit his lip with vexation and trouble, and then, stepping a little to one side, he saw with amazement that the prostrate man was not asleep at all.

His eyes were wide open, and he stared before him. Far in

the distance, the noise of thunder rolled swiftly upon them. And now the red man stretched a hand before him, toward the north, which was the side to which he faced, and broke into a loud chant!

Torridon felt either that he was in the presence of a madman, or that his own wits had gone wrong.

CHAPTER XIX

★

Life Or Death

At the first loud words of that song, as though in answer to them, the gray mare, Comanche, and the tall, black stallion rushed up onto the narrow island, snorting with terror. Ashur, as by instinct, made straight for his master. The mare crowded at his side.

At that the voice of the prostrate Indian was raised to a higher key, and though the words were perfectly unknown to Torridon, he could not help feeling in them terror and exultation combined. For the whole body of the Indian was now pulsing with emotion.

Now the thunder grew, and glancing back over his shoulder, Torridon at last saw the cause of it. He saw a steep wall of water plunging down the northern branch of the river, while the southern fork remained as dry as ever, only a small trickle of water meandering through the center of the bed of sand and pebbles and boulders.

He could remember that in the many tales of Roger Lincoln there had been descriptions of just such floods as this, caused by heavy rainfall in the hills, when the heavens sometimes opened and let down the water in sheets. Sweeping into the courses, sluiced off the naked brown hills, those waters then began a headlong descent, sometimes smashing open beaver dams and adding the treasures of those waters to the original flood.

Among such phenomena this must have been a giant, for the strong gorge was crowded with the water almost to its brim. Out of the frothing current whole trees were flung up, like the arms of a hidden giant rejoicing in his strength, and as the wave plunged on its way, it sliced away the banks on either side, so that a continual swath of trees was topping inwards as though brought down by a pair of incredible scythes.

Whether madman or monster, the prostrate Indian was a human being. What would happen to this tottering little island when the vast wall of water struck it? Already, at the thunderous coming of the flood, the trees trembled; a fissure was opened inside the big tree which leaned out from the bank toward the north.

Torridon caught the sleeper by the naked shoulder and shook him. Under his hand he felt the flesh cold as earth, and covered with an icy damp. And though he shouted and pointed toward the rush of water, the other would not stir. He merely cast out both hands before him and began to shout his chant more loudly than ever.

And then the water struck.

There was an instant visible and audible blow. It shook Torridon so that he almost fell, and the gray mare was flung to her knees. The big tree at the side of the island lurched halfway to a fall, with a sound like the tearing of strong canvas in the hands of a giant as the roots were snapped.

The whole forward point of the land was torn away, and huge arms of yellow spray leaped fifty or a hundred feet in the air. The rain of their descent drenched horse and man, and the air was filled with a sort of brownish mist so that Torridon could see only dimly what followed.

He was sure of death, but he yearned to see death coming clearly.

Then, at his very side, the whole edge of the island went down. Vast froth was boiling at his feet as he staggered back against the side of Ashur. Out of the maddening waters a tree trunk, stripped of its branches in the ceaseless mill of the tumbling flood, was shot up, javelinwise—a ton-weight javelin—flung lightly through the air. It rose, it towered above them, and it fell with a mighty crash—upon the motionless Indian, as Torridon thought in his first horror. And then he saw that the still quivering trunk lay at the head of the red man, its dripping side mere inches away from the skull which it would have crushed like an egg.

And the wall of water was gone. Its thunder departed into the distance with the speed of a galloping horse, and behind it, it left the gorge with a rushing current. The air cleared from the mist. In those currents Torridon could see boulders spinning near the surface like corks. He was more amazed and bewildered by the force in that after current than he had been by the face and forefront of the flood.

Yet the storm of water decreased with wonderful rapidity. In a few moments the gorge was hardly ankle-deep with a sliding, bubbling stream, and the wet, raw edges of the ravine dripped into the currents.

Then Torridon could look around him, and he saw that they stood on a little platform barely large enough to accommodate the two humans and the two horses. In the very center stood one thick-trunked tree, and doubtless its ancient roots, reaching far down, had been the one anchor which the moving waters had been unable to wrench away. Otherwise man and horse must have gone down like straws in that dreadful mill.

The Indian now rose, though with great effort. He staggered, and had to lean a shoulder against the trunk of the tree. Then he threw up both his hands and burst into a chant louder than any he had uttered before. He seemed to be half mad with joy. Sometimes in the midst of his strange singing, laughter swelled in his throat. Tears of extreme joy shone in his eyes.

Torridon would have put the fellow down as a hopeless madman, but something in that ecstatic voice and in the raised head told him that the warrior was speaking to his Creator. It was like a war song of triumph, it was also like a great prayer and a thanksgiving.

As for the meaning, Torridon had no clew, but he waited, determined to be wary and cautious.

"Never take your eyes from a hostile, night or day," said Roger Lincoln. "He'll count coup on you while you're asleep, and take a scalp, even if he can't get a hundred yards away before vengeance overtakes him!"

When the song of the Indian ended, it seemed as though life had ended in him also. He slid down the trunk of the tree until he lay crumpled at its feet. His eyes were open and glaring; there was a faint froth on his lips. Torridon assured himself that the fellow was dead. But when he felt above the heart of the red man, he was aware of a faint pulsation, feeble, and very rapid and uneven. The body which had been so clammy to the touch was now burning with feverish heat. He was not dead, but he was very sick.

Torridon looked from their crumbling island across the long leagues of prairie which stretched on either side of the trees fringing the water course.

The temptation was plain in him to be away from this place and turn his back on the sick man. He knew nothing about such matters, but even a child could have told him that, left unassisted, the other would die before the sun went down.

Then strong conscience took hold on Torridon. He set his teeth and looked about him, determined to fight off that death if he could. If he had been but six months on the plains, he might have had another viewpoint, filled with the prejudices of the trappers and hunters of the frontier, but to him now this was simply a human being with skin that was not white.

First of all he must get the man from the island, and that would not be easy. Then for a safer place to which to take him.

He went down to explore, the stallion and the mare slipping and stumbling after him down the sheer side of the bluff. From the bed of the stream he turned up the southern fork, and he had not gone a hundred yards before he discovered what he wanted— an opening among big trees on its bank, with a promise of present shelter.

He returned to the island, the two horses following close at his heels. The terror through which they had passed was still upon them. No doubt they felt that only the mysterious wisdom of the human had saved them from being caught into the whirl of the waters. Now they crowded at the heels of their protector.

He had to wave them back as he climbed up the slope again.

He found the red man totally unconscious now. It was a limp body that he took into his arms and half carried, half dragged to the verge of the descent. There followed Herculean labor, getting his burden down to the level, but once there the task was much easier. He managed to fold the Indian like a half-filled sack over the back of the mare, because she was lower, and because Ashur no doubt would have bucked off such a burden as often as it was intrusted to him.

But Comanche went cheerfully along under this burden, and she climbed the bank of the southern fork and so brought the sick man to a new home.

The Indian had recovered a little from his trance. The violent jarring and hauling which he had received started him raving. And as Torridon lifted him from the back of the mare the red man uttered a howl like the bay of a hunting wolf.

Torridon almost let his burden fall as he heard that dreadful cry, but afterward the other lay still on the grass, muttering rapidly, his eyes closed, or rolling wildly when they opened.

First of all he was dragged onto a blanket. Then Torridon prepared, with all the haste he could, a bed of branches, made deep and soft as springs, and covered the top with soft sprigs of green.

On this he heaved the Indian with difficulty, for the man was of a big frame, though greatly wasted.

Then there was a shelter to be erected. Torridon had seen enough woodcraft to know something about how it should be built. He had with him a strong hatchet. Rather, it was a broad ax-head, set upon a short haft, and with this he soon felled a number of saplings. The bed he had built close to the trunk of a big and spreading tree. He found a great fallen branch, dead for so long that it was greatly lightened in weight, but still tough and strong. Some fallen limbs rot at once; in others the wood is merely cured. It was all he could do to work the branch near the chosen spot and then to raise its lighter end and lodge it in the fork of the sheltering tree.

This branch now became his ridge-pole. Against it laid the

saplings, and in a surprisingly short time he had a comparatively secure shelter. Afterward, when he had more leisure, he could complete the structure with some sort of thatching. In the meantime he had a place which would shield the sick man from the night air.

It was dark when all this had been done, yet he worked on, taking off the packs, arranging the contents within the "tent" house, and then preparing food.

For his own part, he was ravenously hungry, but when he made a broth of the jerked venison and offered it at the lips of the sick man the latter clenched his teeth and refused all sustenance. Torridon heaved a cruel sigh of relief. It might be that he would be freed from his captivity by the immediate death of the red man.

CHAPTER XX

★

White Thunder

That early hope was not fulfilled.

For three days the Indian raved and raged and muttered day and night. For a week after that his fever was still high. And then it left him.

It left him a helpless wreck, a ghost of a man. His belly clove against his spine. Deep purple hollows lay between the ribs. His face was shrunken mortally. With his sunken eyes and his great arch of a nose and his projecting chin he looked like a cartoon of a predatory monster.

But his wits had returned to him. He lay on the bed and rolled his eyes toward Torridon, and there was, for the first time, sense and life in that glance.

Torridon was enormously cheered. He fell to work with all his might to complete the task which he had pushed forward so far and so well. He had arranged small snares. Out of them he took each day rabbits and small birds, and he cooked little broths and then stronger stews, and the red man ate and gained slowly in strength.

Torridon knew something about the care of fever patients. At least that they must be fed only a little at a time. Certainly he overdid caution and delayed the recovery of the red man's strength, but every step forward was a sure step, and never once did the convalescent beg for more food, even when there was a raging fire of hunger in his eyes.

Weeks passed before he could sit up; a long time before he could stand; many days before he could walk; many more before he could ride.

But that was not an empty time for either of them.

He who is raised with a book in his hand comes to need mental occupation as much as he needs food. As for the hunting, it was easily done. Much game followed the course of the stream, up and down. The work around the camp was small, likewise, and when the brain of the sick man cleared, Torridon spent the remainder of each day with him. And since talk was impossible until he had mastered the language, he set about the study of it.

Never did student make such progress!

He himself had been a school-teacher for four years, cudgeling information into the dull heads of the Bretts. Now he had himself for a pupil and he drove himself remorselessly. He wrote down every word that he heard and memorized it, going patiently over and over the list. There were many sounds which were hard to duplicate with the alphabet. For those sounds he invented symbols. And as he progressed in his talk, he still kept paper at hand and jotted down the corrections which the convalescent red man made.

And, before long, talk could flow freely between them, particularly since, in their conversation, the red man did most of the speaking. For he had much to say, and furthermore, he knew how to say it.

His name was Standing Bull. He was a Cheyenne warrior. In the lodge at home he had two wives and three children. He was young, and he was rising in his tribe, and then trouble came to him. He explained it to Torridon as follows.

Eleven times he had been on the warpath. On these excursions he had been very successful. He had brought back many horses, forty or fifty, according to varying counts, for the narrator seemingly allowed himself some latitude. But, more than horses, he had taken three scalps, and he had counted no fewer than eight coups.

Of this he was enormously proud.

"What is a coup?" asked Torridon, very curious.

"A child with a gun may take the life of a strong warrior from a distance," said the Cheyenne, "or a child with a bow may shoot from the darkness and kill a chief. But when a coup is counted it is different. I charge in a battle. I see an enemy. I have a charge in my rifle, but I do not shoot. No, instead of that I keep the bullet in my gun. I rush my enemy. He fires at me. I stoop and the bullet flies over my head. He snatches out a knife. I swerve away from it and, reaching from my horse, I touch him with my coup stick. It is greater than the killing or the scalping of him."

"But why?" persisted Torridon. "If you kill him then there is one less enemy for you and your people. That is a great advantage. You may say that it proves you are a greater warrior than the other man!"

"That is true," smiled the Cheyenne. "The white men are wise and do clever things. They do many things that the Indian cannot do. The Indian cannot make guns, for instance. Well, still Heammawihio gives the red man some gifts which he does not give to the white man. He gives him understanding of many things. That is only right and fair. You would not want the white man to have all the understanding, White Thunder?"

That was the name he had given to Torridon. Because, apparently, he had come into the life of the Cheyenne with a white face, and on the wings of the thundering rush of water that so nearly carried them all into another life.

"No," agreed Torridon. "Of course the Indians have understanding."

"And the most important thing of all is the counting of coups!"

"How can that be?" said Torridon, amazed.

"Look!" said the warrior. "What is the greatest thing you wish to have?"

Torridon thought only a moment.

"A good woman," he said.

It was the time when the Cheyenne was halfway toward his natural strength. He could raise himself on his elbows in order to look his companion straight in the face.

When he made sure that Torridon was not jesting he lay down again with a murmur that was half a grunt.

"Women," he said at last, "can be bought for horses, or for beads. Women are very good," he added hastily, for he always showed the greatest tact in saving the feelings of the white man, "because they cook and keep the lodge clean and fresh, they flesh hides and cure them, they make clothes, and above all, they may bear man children. But, nevertheless, there are other things you white men want! What are they?"

"We want money, I suppose," said Torridon, who found it rather difficult to look at life in such a naked fashion. When he looked inward, he hardly knew what would evolve from the mist.

"Money, money!" said the Cheyenne almost harshly. "Well, you want women for wives, and you want money. What else?"

"To do something important."

"Like what?" said the warrior.

"Like—well, building a great house, say. Or making beautiful pictures."

Standing Bull was hardly able to suppress his scorn.

"A great lodge," he said, "is very well. It is good for little children and for women, and for old men, of course. But for young braves there is no need of a better lodge than this!"

Torridon thought at first that the other meant the wretched shelter in which he then lay. The leaves of the branches had withered now, and with the passage of every wind there was a sad hushing from the crumbling house of leaves. But then Torridon understood that the gesture of the Cheyenne indicated things beyond—the wide blue dome of the sky—it was the evening of the day—and the dim mountains and pillars of cloud beneath it.

He had no answer to this remark. It was hardly possible that he could explain the beauty of architecture to the red man.

"As for paintings," went on the Indian, "it is true that they are good, too, on a lodge. A wise painter lets the spirits know that they are reverenced. Also, the colors are pleasant to the eye. But though paintings are sacred and pleasant, I never have seen a painted buffalo that looked as much like a real buffalo as this withered branch looks like a whole strong tree planted in the ground."

"There are other kinds of painting," suggested Torridon.

The Cheyenne overrode this suggestion with a sweep of his arm in which the muscles were beginning to grow again.

"I ask you what you want and you speak of women, money, lodges, paint. Now let me tell you what the Indian wants. He does not want to have many women. Just enough to do the work in his lodge. He does not care for money or for more than a few painted robes to hang on his lodge. But he cares for something else. What he wants to have is many souls!"

He paused, triumphantly staring at the white man.

"I rush in toward my enemy, I avoid his bullet. I take the cut of his knife in order to touch him with my coup stick. Because, when I do that, some of his soul runs up the stick and passes all over me, and nobody can wash away that new soul which I have stolen. It is mine! I, Standing Bull, have counted eight coups. Who will say, then, that my soul has not been made greater and stronger?"

"What makes you so sure of that?" asked Torridon. "Though I know that you are a brave man, Standing Bull, still I think that the three braves you have killed and scalped are a greater proof of your courage than all your coups!"

The Cheyenne smiled and closed his eyes a moment, a sign that he was thinking hard. At last he shook his head.

"Do you know that our word for white man has two meanings?" he asked.

"Yes," said Torridon. "I know that you use the same word for spider and for white man."

"This is the reason," said the Cheyenne. "The spider is more cunning than all other things. It can walk on the air. It can hang in the wind. So does the white man. He, too, can do strange things. He even has thunder canoes, I have heard, though that is hard to believe. But you see that there are some things that the white man cannot understand, and that he cannot do. Well, counting of coups is one of them.

"But you, White Thunder, stay with me a long time and listen to me. When I go back to my people I am going to make a scalp shirt, and then I shall be a chief. The young men will follow me, also. Now you are a wise white man. I shall make you a wise Indian. And when you are that, then who will be so wise and so great in the world as White Thunder?"

He paused and made a little gesture, palm up. It was as though he had offered to Torridon his own soul in the palm of his hand!

CHAPTER XXI

★

Men, Women, And Horses

There was only one thing that seriously overclouded their relations, and that was when Torridon told the Cheyenne that he could not remain with him very long, but, as soon as the warrior's strength had come back, Torridon must make the best of his way across the plains to find Fort Kendry.

When he first asked after Fort Kendry the Cheyenne had let him understand that he himself knew the way to it perfectly and could direct him so clearly that a child traveling by night could have found the place. But when he understood his companion's fixed determination of going there, Standing Bull grew sullen and even angry.

"Why should you go to the Fort?" he asked. "What is there for you except what they have taken from the poor Indians? But when you go there, you will have to pay for the things that are there."

He added bitterly: "White men do not give away for nothing. They want money and many robes." He added, by way of coating this bitter comment with sugar: "No one is so clever as a white man. You will not gain when you trade with them, White Thunder!"

"I don't want guns or robes," said Torridon patiently. "I only want to find a girl there."

"Ha!" cried the Cheyenne. "A woman!"

"She is promised to me as my wife," said Torridon.

"A woman! A woman!" repeated the Indian, and then closed

Coward of the Clan ☆ 119

his eyes as though to check a torrent of scorn which was ready to burst forth from his lips.

"Tell me, my brother," he said at last, "is this woman young? Or is she an old squaw with many robes and horses?"

"She is young," said Torridon. He smiled a little and then added: "She has no robes or horses. None at all, I suppose."

"She is strong, then?" said the warrior. "She knows how to flesh skins and how to make soft moccasins and how to bead and do quill work?"

"I don't think she understands any of those things," said the white man. "Certainly she isn't big or strong. She's very small."

Again the Cheyenne was forced to close his eyes.

"Her father promised her to you? Then he was lucky to find a brave who would take such a—woman."

Obviously he had left out the word "worthless" in his pause. He added: "Is she plain, or pretty?"

"She?" said Torridon. Then his breast heaved and his heart swelled. He was talking to a wild Indian, but he had been silent for a long time. "She is the most beautiful creature that ever was made."

"So?" said the warrior. "Then long before this some other brave has come and taken her. If you offered five horses for her, he has offered ten. She is gone to his tepee. Think no more about her. A woman cannot make the heart of a great brave sore for many days. Very soon he takes another squaw. If you want wives, you shall have them. When you come home with me to my people I shall find you the daughters of great chiefs. I shall pay the horses to buy them for you. I shall fill your tepee with everything that you need. Then you will be happy?"

He smiled expectantly, and Torridon was forced to answer slowly: "There is no other who can take her place." He added: "Any other woman would be horrible to me!"

"Look at me while I speak the truth with a straight tongue," said the Cheyenne. "One woman has strong hands and fleshes many robes. Another knows how to do bead work swiftly and well. Yes, there is a difference between women. But take two wives in the place of this single one."

Torridon hunted through his mind. He saw that it was useless to delve into the mysteries of love with this man.

"You have many horses?" he asked at last.

"Many—many—" said the warrior, smiling with pride.

"Are they all the same?"

"No. There is a bay stallion which is worth all the rest."

"Look at me," echoed Torridon. "I speak with a straight tongue, too. Your stallion, I think, is worth all the rest. Perhaps, however, he is not worth as much as that gray mare?"

He pointed to Comanche, which was grazing near by. And as though she knew she was under discussion, she lifted her lovely head and looked toward them with confidence and affection. The Cheyenne regarded her with a burning glance.

"It is true, it is true!" he muttered, as one who had had that thought often in his mind before.

Torridon whistled. Black Ashur came bounding and stood before them.

"But," said Torridon, "though this mare is very fast, Ashur leaves her standing behind him. Though she is very strong, he will run twice as far as she can run. Though she has a great heart, he will die for me!"

"Is it true?" asked the Cheyenne, the same greedy fire in his eyes. "Yes, it is true," he answered himself with conviction, "because he has the eye of a chief. Like a chief in council he holds his head. And he runs on the wind. My brother is a great chief among the white men, or he would not have two such horses!"

"Now," went on Torridon, "if there is such a difference between horses, can there not be such a difference between women?"

"Certainly not," replied Standing Bull with warmth. "Does a woman carry a brave to battle? Is his life depending on her? Does she give him the speed to run away from danger? Does she give him the speed to overtake his enemy and strike him down? No, no, White Thunder, you are very wise. All white men are wise. But this is a thing about which you will grow older!"

Coward of the Clan ☆ 121

Torridon gave up the debate with a shrug of his shoulders, for he saw that he was facing a wall of rock.

They talked of many other things in the days which followed.

Finally he began to support Standing Bull from the shelter and out under the open sky, and lead him to a blanket where he could sit for hours, drinking up the strength-giving sun and breathing deeply of the pure air.

He was a huge man, standing. He was two or three inches over six feet, with great, spreading shoulders, and arms of an almost unnatural length, set off with huge hands which Torridon could hardly look upon without a shudder of fear. In the old days he had known only two men who impressed him so much. One was Roger Lincoln. But that hero was like Achilles, formidable rather in skill and speed, and graceful surety of all his ways. He was strong, also, but not a giant of power. A giant of power was Jack Brett. He had shoulders as massive as those of the Cheyenne. Perhaps hard labor and the carrying of packs through the woods had given him even a greater force than that of the Indian warrior, but Standing Bull had something of the speed and grace of Roger Lincoln united with the massive might of hand of Jack Brett.

Rarely could an uglier face than the Indian's have been found, with its great, predatory nose; its wide, thin, cruel lips; the eyes, buried, small, terribly bright and restless, and the chin curving well out. He looked like a very god of battle, and as such Torridon looked upon him.

Lying prone in the shelter of the house of leaves, he could care for and pity Standing Bull, but once the giant was erect and walking, in spite of himself Torridon was daily more and more afraid. He remembered, with increasing frequency and force, the warnings which he had received from Roger Lincoln—an Indian never must be trusted to the hilt. Give him hope, watch him, use him when you can, but recall that always he is as treacherous as a snake.

Torridon, hearing those warnings in the old days, had come to feel that red men were men in form only. And these warnings had been reinforced by stories of midnight massacres, rum-inspired outpourings of murder and cruelty and frightfulness. And all these tales rolled up in his mind and he believed them all when he looked upon the terrible form and face of the Cheyenne.

The very voice of the warrior was like a roll of drums, a heavy bass that reverberated. And when Standing Bull stood outside the tent and shouted with joy because of the goodness of the sun as it burned upon his thin face, Torridon shook as though thunder had pealed in his ear.

At last a day came when the warrior was seen walking beside Ashur, while the latter regarded him cautiously from a corner of his eye.

"Tell me, brother, which horse shall I ride when we go back to my people?"

"Which will you have, Standing Bull?"

"The gray horse is a strong and a wonderful horse. She runs as fast as leaping lightning, but she is not like the black stallion. Only to sit on his back across the plains to the tepees of my people—"

Torridon smiled.

"The black horse is like black thunder. He is full of strength and wickedness, Standing Bull."

"Good," said the warrior. "Saddle him and you will see that I fit the saddle!"

It was his way of saying that no horse could throw him. Torridon half believed that he was right, and he was worried. Once the brave felt the magic of Ashur beneath him, would he be persuaded except by a greater force than Torridon could show, to part from the stallion?

However, now he was committed, and he saddled Ashur with care, and lengthened the stirrups to fit the great legs of the chief. He stood at the head of the horse and watched the Cheyenne leap into his seat.

"Now," said Standing Bull.

Ashur crouched like a cat.

"Be wary!" warned Torridon, and stepped back.

Wary was the other.

Nobly, nobly, in another day, Roger Lincoln had sat on the back of that same Ashur, until flung senseless to the ground. The Cheyenne rode in another manner. He was like a panther clutching the back of a wounded bull. And it seemed to Torridon that Ashur had found a master of sheer force at last.

Yet there was an undiscovered spirit in the stallion. He seemed to expand in size, in force, as the seconds flew. He grew a flashing black monster, more in the air than on the ground. And at last, out of a whirl of bucking, out of a dizzy spinning, the Cheyenne emerged headfirst through the cloud of dust, rolled over and over, and then lurched drunkenly to his feet. Blood was running from ears, nose, mouth. But he laughed.

"It is true," he said. "Heammawihio has made such a horse for only one man. Take him, my brother! I am smaller, now. I shall sit on the gray mare!"

And he laughed again, in the most perfect good nature.

CHAPTER XXII

★

Medicine To Be Made

This was the reason that, when they started back over the plains for the Cheyenne village, the Indian was on the gray mare, Comanche. He was hugely delighted with her, and taking her for a racing course in the most headlong style, he came plunging back to Torridon and assured him that there was nothing among the horses of the Cheyennes that could keep pace with her. He even invited Torridon to race the stallion against the gray, but Torridon put off the suggestion.

He was very willing to believe that Standing Bull felt great obligations to him as a deliverer in time of need; but he could not help remembering the many tales of Roger Lincoln; and sometimes the warrior looked at Ashur with such glittering eyes that Torridon almost felt a knife planted in the small of his back. So he refused to race against the mare, and when Standing Bull let her stretch away faster and faster—when they were cantering side by side—he allowed the mare to go off into the lead and refused to let Ashur measure strides with her.

Eventually Standing Bull gave up his curiosity. Instead, he returned to the tale of the thing that had sent him out to lie on the island by the side of the river. Several times before he had begun the narration, but always had broken off, letting himself be diverted from the point of his talk like a man who is unwilling to tell of things which are too unpleasant.

What had happened, as Torridon eventually found out, was that Standing Bull, in the midst of his rising glory as a fighter, had returned with a war party and found a party of Sioux blocking their way. In the skirmish that followed, all was going well until Standing Bull, giving way to an ecstasy of battle glory, charged in among the Dakotas and tried to count coup on one of the chief braves among the Sioux.

He almost had succeeded, and he grew tense with grief and trouble when he recalled that he had been so close to endless glory. But the Sioux had swayed from the charge and managed to reach the head of Standing Bull with a stroke with the butt end of his rifle.

It floored Standing Bull.

When he came to he found the Dakotas had been forced to retreat before they had a chance to take his scalp or settle him with a knife thrust. But by the time the singing was gone out of his head he discovered that he had lost that which was more precious to him than the very hair on his head—his medicine bag!

He and all the party had searched the ground where the battle was fought. They had scanned every crevice. But the bag was gone and poor Standing Bull was in a frightful state of mind.

"But what is a medicine bag?" asked Torridon.

"The soul of a brave!" said the warrior, and would not explain any further.

However, Torridon in the past had heard enough references to the medicine bag to make him understand that the Indians actually felt the immaterial soul of a warrior was connected with his medicine bag.

With his "soul" gone from him, Standing Bull found that all his former achievements were looked upon as lost with the medicine bag. He would not be accepted as a member of a war party. His voice would not be heard in the council. And he determined that something desperate must be undertaken in order to change the condition of his life.

The medicine men and the wise sages of the tribe could not advise him. He determined, therefore, to leave the tribe and go forth to make new medicine with the help of the spirits. As a young man goes to consult the future, so Standing Bull went out to lie in danger until a sign was given to him.

He had selected the little island where the river forked. It was considered an enchanted spot. Here he lay for four days, never turning from his right side. At last came the thunder of the water; the white man and the two horses rushed up to him; and Standing Bull's soul was filled with joy, for he felt that this was indeed a direct sign from heaven.

To Torridon this story seemed at once amusing, pathetic, and worthy of inspiring fear. He could understand, after he had heard it, that attitude of the Cheyenne toward him, as though he were a personal possession of Standing Bull, and all that he had with him a part of the property of the brave. Heaven had brought him to Standing Bull. Therefore, being from heaven, he must be treated with respect, consideration, gentleness; but at the same time he belonged to Standing Bull; he had been given to Standing Bull in a dream straight from heaven, a dream so powerful that it had not faded as other visions are apt to fade, but had materialized into flesh and blood and iron!

It was easy, too, to understand why Standing Bull had disliked the thought that Torridon wanted to go to Fort Kendry. Furthermore, it was not really right that a man from heaven should want to go to any place other than the abode of the brave to whom he had been sent as a material dream.

It made a situation so ludicrous that Torridon could have burst into laughter. It made a situation so grave that he was ready to quake with fear.

He had serious thoughts of making an attack upon his companion and then riding off to take his chance on the prairie, but the prairie to him was as unknown as the uncharted sea, and, besides, to attack the warrior would have been no less difficult than to attack a wolf. He slept with one eye open; he was ever on the alert; and Torridon began to submit to his fate with a growing apprehension of what it might lead him to.

So they voyaged across the plains. The weather was clear. Sometimes little clouds of purest crystal white, filled with brilliance, blew rapidly across the sky; otherwise it was washed clear. And all day the heat was blinding and burning in its intensity, and the face of the plains quivered with the heat waves that danced endlessly upwards. Often from the burning of the sun against his shoulders, Torridon groaned, and then his big companion would look sharply at him.

"Speak louder, louder, brother!" he would say. "When the spirits wish to use your tongue, speak with a loud voice, so that I may hear!"

Torridon would only shake his head and declare that it was only the heat of the sun, but when he said this, Standing Bull merely smiled a little, secret smile, as though he knew a great deal, and would not press the subject with too many questions. He was willing to be patient with his strange captive.

In the heart of Torridon there was that mingled fear and curious expectancy which filled the old explorers, sailing for the first time through unknown seas; and he turned pale when, on a day, Standing Bull raised his arm and pointed into the eye of the sun. Beneath the sun, like a thickening of the horizon mist, thin clouds were rising—smoke!

"It is there," said Standing Bull. "Presently we shall see our people!"

The confusion in the Cheyenne's mind was revealed by that speech. In part he looked on Torridon simply as a white man. In part, the white man was a messenger from heaven, a bringer of luck and medicine to him. And, in part, Torridon was actually a Cheyenne himself, because he had been sent down by the Great Spirit to that tribe.

To a logical and educated mind the three points of view would have been impossible, of course. But Standing Bull could separate the three thoughts. He used them one by one and looked upon his companion in the fashion which was most convenient at the moment.

Presently Standing Bull checked the grey mare. He gestured before him where arose a few swellings of the ground.

"Shall I cross the hills and ride in to the village?" he asked.

"You know what is best to do," said Torridon.

The warrior exclaimed impatiently: "Why do you keep back your knowledge, White Thunder? Do you wish to do me harm? Or do you think that Standing Bull is a fool? No, no! I am not a fool. I know that you have understanding of everything. Otherwise, why did Heammawihio send you to me? Now, be kind to me and tell me what I should do.'

Torridon half closed his eyes. But he saw that it was useless to argue and protest. To Standing Bull he was a miraculous creature. He consulted, therefore, his own disinclination to go into the Cheyenne village.

"We should wait here," he said at last.

The brave smiled with satisfaction.

"They will come out to find me, will they not?" he said. "They will come out and escort me into the city? They will give me honor, White Thunder?"

"They will," sighed Torridon.

Standing Bull in a vast excitement dismounted, took out his paints, and straightway began to blacken his face. Next he brushed out the mane and the tail of the gray mare. He rubbed away the dust which covered the bead and quillwork on his moccasins and leggings. He combed out his long hair over his shoulders, and he began to put added touches of improvement, such as streaks of paint on his brawny arms. In a few moments he was a brilliant and terrible form, and Torridon looked upon him with awe.

"My heart is filled with impatience, White Thunder!" exclaimed the brave. "Send them out to me soon!"

He hardly had spoken when a boy riding without a saddle galloped a horse over the verge of the hill, swept toward them, and then with a sudden shout wheeled his horse and rushed away. Standing Bull could not speak. He was throttled by emotion and literally bared his teeth like a wolf as he waited.

He was on his horse again, wrapped in his buffalo robe, magnificent and grim, when a cavalcade of half a dozen warriors came over the hill and galloped toward them. The Cheyennes spread out suddenly in a fan, and with a war yell they charged. Torridon glanced at his companion, but he saw a faint smile on the lips of Standing Bull—a smile which that hero was struggling to suppress.

A rush of horsemen, a sweeping cloud of dust, and then they

wheeled and came up. Keen glances they flung at Torridon; he felt his scalp prickling on his head!

"Brother!" cried a magnificent youth who seemed the leader of the six riders. "You come with your face blackened. Have you taken a scalp with no harm to yourself? And have you brought this prisoner back with you?"

"Rising Hawk," said the other. "I have been on such a trail as no Cheyenne ever walked or rode before. But this is not the time to speak of it. There is medicine to be made before another word can pass my lips!"

CHAPTER XXIII

★

Fierce Welcome

There was a murmur of eager contentment among the others. They seemed to accept the fact that this was a mystery about to be carried into their encampment. Four remained as a sort of guard of honor; two raced their horses off over the hill, and by the time that Torridon with the others had climbed to the crest, there was a stream of rapid riders swinging out toward him.

He saw a village of lofty tepees which flashed clean as metal against the sun, and between them and the village was a river, fallen very low. The flats on either side of the stream were covered with corn, but so dust sprinkled that it was hardly visible to the eye at the first glance. Only by the margin of the stream was it a strong green, as though there it had been irrigated.

Out from the big circle of the town riders were breaking, men, women, boys, little girls. Each horse, as it struck the shallow stream, sent a white dash of spray flying high, and then the rider lurched on up the nearer bank.

Torridon felt that the end of the world was flying upon him. The riders came in a vast tide of noise, with arms brandished. Guns exploded. Wild whoops cut at his ears. And around him poured the tribe.

A huge warrior, naked to the waist, drove straight at him with ax lifted, the sun flashing on it. That flash glanced in the very eyes of Torridon. But the blow was not driven home. The brave went on by with a war yell that stunned the brain of Torridon, and in place of the ax wielder, a spearsman was galloping, bent low over the mane of his horse, and with his lancepoint leveled at the breast of the white man. This time, surely, the steel would slide home through his breast. No, at the last instant the point was raised, glanced over his shoulder, and another terrible cry dinned in his ears. A procession of terrible forms rushed against him and went by, leaving him untouched. Then a naked boy was dancing beside him, threatening him with a knife whose blade was at least a foot long, and sharpened to an airy edge.

Torridon felt that devils had flooded the world! He would have shrunk from this terrible peril, but his nerves were as numb as though paralyzed.

He heard the exultant voice of Standing Bull beside him: "My brother is fearless. He who has ridden down from the sky on the white thunder, what would make him tremble on the earth!"

He could not answer this friendly and proud remark. If he opened his lips he felt that a scream would come from them.

The riders had formed in a vast, irregularly eddying circle. Dust clouds boiled up. Through the dust he saw the frantic shapes gleaming, men like polished forms of bronze, terrible in action.

And, slowly, they moved on—they the focus and the center of the storm. They crossed the creek. They entered the village, they were pushing through solid masses of horses, men, dogs, which writhed away before them and closed again behind. The heat became intense. Dust choked Torridon. A knife thrust between the ribs would have been a happy ending to this prologue of terror and burning sun and confusion.

A woman screamed above the din. She was a young squaw, holding an infant boy high above her head, a naked little statue of red-gold in the flash of the sun. Standing Bull did not so much as turn his head, and yet Torridon knew, by instinct, that they had passed one of the wives of the brave.

Before them the crowd began to split; there were warriors working with a sort of organization to push the rest to either side, and so a way was opened to the front of the biggest tepee which Torridon yet had seen. It was painted yellow below, and black above, spotted with little yellow crosses, and on either side of the doorway buffalo bulls were painted with a good deal of skill, and above the doorway a green crescent moon.

In front of the lodge stood a very old man. The arm with which he held his buffalo robe about him was withered like the arm of a mummy. The flesh was gone from his face, but instead of making him look wrinkled and old, the skin was stretched a little, like parchment. It gave him rather the look of a starved boy than of an old man, and the eyes were bright and bold as the eyes of a child.

Before this ancient Standing Bull dismounted, and greeted him with the greatest respect. Torridon himself was motioned from his horse and dismounted. His knees sagged under him. A breath would have staggered him, so completely was he unnerved. He felt reasonably sure of death. He would almost have welcomed such an ending, but it was the means which he had in his mind like a nightmare. He had heard the great Roger Lincoln tell of Indian tortures, of splinters thrust under the nails of the victim, and then lighted; of the tearing and shaving away of flesh; of slow roasting over fires.

Those were the images which drifted rapidly between the eyes of Torridon and the strange forms around him. He hardly knew how he was brought into the tepee. But there he found himself seated, with Standing Bull beside him. The old chief, called High Wolf, who seemed to be the head of the tribe, sat facing the doorway. Presently others entered. Finally ten men had come in, each carefully passing behind the backs of the others, avoiding moving before any one, until they came to a place where they could sit. They were like ten senators at council. Torridon did not need to be told that the ten chief men of the tribe had gathered here for deliberation of some sort. The youngest among them were Standing Bull and that graceful brave, Rising Hawk, who first had come out to meet them.

Outside, the noise was dying down, but when the lodge flap was dropped, the dust clouds were still rising. It was hot in the lodge, although the lower edges had been furled to admit the passage of a draft. It was hot because of the intense sun beating down from above, and because, also, of the fire which burned in a heart-shaped excavation in the center of the lodge with a steaming kettle on it.

"Everything is here," said High Wolf. "You may eat."

Standing Bull raised his hand, big as a shield, heavy as metal.

"First we must be purified," said he. "Every one here must be purified. There is a great medicine in this lodge, High Wolf."

The old man glanced at Standing Bull. The turning of his eyes was like the stirring of two red lights, but Torridon guessed shrewdly that it was pleasure that moved the great chief.

He himself then took wisps of sweet grass, ignited them, and waving the smoke to the earth, to the sky, to the four corners of the heavens, he muttered a chant so rapidly that Torridon could not understand the words. Then he carried the smoke to all the guests. They washed their hands in it. This, apparently, was a degree of purification.

Still the ceremonies were not ended. Five small pieces of meat were taken from the pot, and one placed in the palm of High Wolf's hand, and the other four at the four points of the compass. Then, inverting his hand upon the palm of his left, he allowed the meat to remain there and offered it to the four directions.

The eating began after that. Torridon found a large portion of unsalted buffalo flesh before him. He ate it greedily. He hoped that food would give him sufficient strength to put an end to the faint tremor which was running steadily through his body.

It did not take long to consume the food. After that the pipe was produced by High Wolf. He filled it with a preparation of tobacco and dried leaves of the sumach, flavored with buffalo grease. After that he blew smoke to the earth, to the heavens, and to the four points of the compass, murmuring a phrase with each puff. Then he passed it to his left. So it went to the door, but apparently it could not cross the doorway, and was passed rapidly back from man to man so that it could begin again on the farther side.

This smoking was done with absorption, without speech, and each man held the pipe in a way which differed slightly from that of others.

At last it was empty.

High Wolf turned to Standing Bull.

"Brother," said he, "Heammawihio is a stern master, but he always is just. We were all sorry when you lost your medicine bag. We wondered what you had done that was wrong. Now we hope that it was taken away from you only in order to inspire you to do some great thing. I think you are about to tell what the great thing may be. We are all ready to hear. We all are your friends. To me you are as a child. Therefore, open your heart and we will receive all your words."

After this courteous invitation all eyes turned upon Standing Bull, and Torridon saw that the braves were in an actual fever of excitement.

That huge warrior, however, remained silent for some time, staring at the ground, and then raised his head on its bull neck and glared up through the smoke hole toward the sun-whitened sky above them.

Then he picked from the floor of the tepee just before him a small handful of little pebbles and grains of sand. This he spread smoothly on the flat of his palm, and then puffed it away. There remained two little glittering pebbles, and these he carefully put away in his pouch.

It seemed to Torridon that this was the maddest sort of nonsense, but all the other braves watched it with the most absorbed attention and respect.

"Now," said Standing Bull, "I have asked the spirits of the air and the under-earth spirits to listen to me. If I say anything that is not true, may they strike me with as many knives as there are grains of dust in that which I have just blown off my hand. If I say the thing which is not true, may they strike me with as many arrows as there were grains of dust, also."

He paused and looked about him from face to face, and every one of those dignified warriors inclined his head a little as though acknowledging the tremendous force of this oath.

"For the thing I am about to tell," said Standing Bull, "is hard to understand. I am going to tell you how I sent my soul up to the Sky People, and how my soul came back again with this man and the two horses and all that was with them besides!"

CHAPTER XXIV

★

A Story Of Truth

Up to this point Torridon had remained more interested in the possibilities of his future fate than in the talk around him, but at his prodigious lie he could not help glancing down sharply to the ground, prepared to hear the outburst of laughter which would greet the statement of Standing Bull.

But there was not a sound!

And when he glanced up again he saw that there was not the slightest indication of mirth in any face. With eyes overbright, the warriors listened, hanging on the words that were next to be spoken. Standing Bull was in no hurry. As one prepared to allow his audience to grow expectant because he had plenty with which to satisfy that expectation, Standing Bull was again looking down to the ground. Or perhaps it might be said that his attitude was that of a man rapt in thought, forgetting those around him while he called up again a vision from the past.

At length he slowly lifted his hand, palm up, and extended his long, powerful arm toward the heavens. Then he said: "When I last saw you, my friends, I was less than a man. My soul was in the hands of the Dakotas. Or else it was rotting on the desert in the rains and drying to dust in the suns. I went out to find another soul.

"I had lain down and asked for a dream and the dream only told me to go out from among my people and follow an invisible guide. I saw no guide, but still I was led for a great distance. I was not told to take a horse, and therefore I left a horse behind me. I did not say farewell to my children or to my wives. I let everything stay behind. Nothing matters to a man so much as his soul!"

Here he paused. He lowered the arm which had been raised as though invoking divine witness to the truth of his words. He went on, after a moment: "I was led through many days of marching. But though I had little food, I was not hungry and I was not tired. I was supported by the thing that led me. At last I came to the place where the great river comes to a fork, and above the fork it has two arms. One arm goes north and the other arm goes west. Where they meet, there is an island."

He paused and looked about him for confirmation.

Rising Hawk said gravely: "I myself have seen that island in the last seven days."

"Do you know what it is now?" asked Standing Bull.

"I know," said Rising Hawk, and said no more, as though he intended to keep his information secret until the end of the tale, thereby being prepared to check its correctness. This made all heads turn for an instant toward Rising Hawk. Excitement apparently was rising fast. This story would be corroborated or completely disproved by an adequate witness!

"Good!" said Standing Bull. "I do not say the thing which is not true. Therefore I am glad that Rising Hawk has seen the place. But when I came to it the spirit that conducted me told me to stay there and lie down. I lay down on my right side, with my head to the east and with my face to the north. I lay on my right side for a long time, waiting for something to happen.

"After a while I began to grow hungry, but more than the hunger was the thirst, and that thirst was like a fire in me, and all the while I could hear the running of the water among the stones in the bed of the river. Sometimes I fell asleep and dreamed that I was the bed of the river and that the cool water was running through my mouth. But I always waked up and found that I still lay on the hard ground. And my bones began to press through my flesh. My muscles asked me to turn, only a little bit, because they were dying.

"Still I would not turn. I did not want to get up and go away.

I did not care to live if I had no soul. All at once, in the middle of a sleep, a voice said to me: 'Stand up and follow me!'

"I knew that it was a spirit. I tried to get up, but I was too weak to move.

"Then the spirit said: 'Your body cannot get up, so leave it behind you.'

"Then I tried to throw out my thought after the spirit, and all at once I felt as though my body were falling down through thin air. The next moment I was standing on my feet. I looked down, and in the starlight I saw that I was still lying on the ground.

"Then I knew that my soul had come away from my body. I heard the spirit call again. I walked. And at one step I crossed to the farther bank of the river. I could see the spirit now. It was an old man with feathers in his hair. He had the ghost of a warbow and stone-pointed arrows in his hand, and the ghost of a painted robe was flying over his shoulders in the wind. He smiled and reached out his hand.

" 'Come with me,' he said.

"He began to walk up through the air. I followed him, and it was as easy to walk up through the air as it was to walk along the ground. Every step we took was longer than the width of this camp.

"After a while we came to the tops of some mountains and we sat down to rest. We could see all the rivers spread out at our feet. Only, to the north and east, there was a shadow on the earth.

"I said to my guide: 'What is that?'

" 'It is the land of the Dakotas,' he answered me.

"Then we stood up and walked through the air again, always going higher, until we reached the clouds. Our bodies were so light that it was rather hard work to walk through them. It was like going in mud. At last we came to the top of the clouds and I saw the sky country filled with Sky People."

He paused again and looked down with a frown. There was a most breathless silence while the others attended this strange narration. Torridon looked to the chief, expecting that his superior intelligence and experience would at once penetrate the deceit, but instead, the nostrils of the old man were quivering and his hollow chest heaved with a passionate joy and belief.

"When I try to remember what was up there," said Standing Bull with a sort of baffled dignity, "my mind walks through darkness. However, I met many good Indians up there. I remember I heard a sound like ten thousand warriors all shouting for battle. I asked what it was and they told me that it was the sound of the wind whistling through the robe of Heammawihio as he strides across the sky country. I remember, too, that I stood before a man as tall as a mountain. He looked like a mountain when it turns blue in the evening. I kneeled before him and begged him to give me another soul. He said that he would. His voice was like the sound of a great river after the spring floods have begun. He offered me a soul in the palm of his hand, but I said: 'If I go back and say that that is my new soul, my people will not believe me. Give me a soul that they can see.'

"After a while he said: 'You ask for a great deal, but I want to please you. You have fought bravely. I have watched you in the field and I never saw you turn away from an equal enemy. Now I am going to make a soul for you!'

"He took up what looked like white clay and began to work it with his fingers, like an old woman molding a pot. After a while he leaned and breathed on it, and there was a sound like a nation singing. After that the lump of clay stood up, breathed, spoke, and was a man."

The narrator turned to Torridon.

"It was this man!" he said.

There was a stir, an intake of breath like a groan. Torridon saw beads of moisture standing on the forehead of Rising Hawk. Not a shadow of disbelief appeared on any face. These people, more simple than children, did not have to be told that it was a fairy tale they were hearing. They were willing to believe with a wonderful faith.

" 'This is your soul!' said Heammawihio to me. 'You had better go down to the earth at once. You had better hurry. The under-water people are very angry because I am helping you. They want to have you and now they are sending down water devils who will destroy your body. If your body is destroyed, of course this new soul will be no good to you!'

"Then he showed me where a white-headed flood was racing down the river toward the island where my body lay.

"I said: 'Alas, we never can get to the body in time!'

" 'That is true,' said the voice. 'Then you must have horses to ride.'

"I saw his hand reach away like the shadow of a cloud that reaches across a valley in a moment. The shadow came back and put two horses beside us. One horse was like silver. One was as black as night.

" 'Which horse will you take?' asked the voice.

"I looked at the white mare. She was like silver. I said that I would take her.

" 'You are wrong,' said Heammawihio, 'because the black stallion is much better than she. But they are both medicine horses. However, you chose the silver mare, and therefore you must keep her and always let your soul ride on the black stallion. Now you must go, and you had better hurry. When you come safely back to the Cheyennes tell them that they are my people. The air that I breathe is sweet with the smoke that they blow up to me!'

"When he had said this, my soul and I got on the horses. They were only the ghosts of horses. We jumped them off the edge of a cloud and they went down like birds. But when I looked before me, I could see a great distance away, because the sun was shining now. I saw the island. I saw my body lying on it, and I saw the flood coming down faster than we could go.

"I said to my soul: 'What shall we do?' He said to me: 'Call to the white thunder!'

"Then I called, and a terrible noise took hold of us, and white thunder wrapped us around, and suddenly we were standing on the island. I looked about me and found my body, and I got into it.

"When I opened my eyes the flood was almost on the island. I looked around me. To the eyes of my spirit, the two horses and the new soul had been as real as this knife!''

He snatched a long weapon from his belt and buried it in the earth with a powerful gesture. Then he went on: "But when I looked at them with the dim eyes of a man they were no more solid than the shapes of mist that come out of the ground on a moonlight evening. But every moment they got thicker and more real. I sang a song to them and told them to hurry and help me, because I was too weak to move. All at once they turned into two real horses and a real man. He caught me up.

"Then the flood struck the island. It tore away almost all of it. It tore away the ground that I had been lying on. It made a noise like thunder, and I could hear the under-water devils groaning and shouting with anger because they could not have my body.

"Then White Thunder, which is the name of this man that the Great Spirit sent down with me, took me away and took care of me while I lay very sick, with all my blood turned into fire. After that, when he had made me strong again with his magic and his strong medicine, we rode back to my people."

He paused again, sat up to his stiffest, fullest height, and looked across at Rising Hawk.

"Friend," he said, "this is a meeting of the great men of the Cheyennes. Every one should hear only the truth. If you have seen the island, speak and let them know if I have said the thing which is not!"

Torridon waited, breathless. Rising Hawk swallowed and then struck the arch of his chest until it resounded like a drum.

"I have seen that island within seven suns," he declared. "It was half as big as this village. There were many trees on it. But when I looked at it again, I saw that it was torn to pieces. All that was left of it was one tree standing, and even the roots of that one tree were washed bare on the north side! So I give my witness that we have heard the truth from our brother!"

CHAPTER XXV

★

Drought

After the conclusion of this short speech from Rising Hawk every one seemed to take it for granted that no further proof was needed. Rising Hawk had seen that the island at the fork of the river actually had been almost destroyed. That was enough, apparently, to verify all the odd tales which Standing Bull had told.

He, like a hero overcome by the mere thought of what he had been through, allowed himself to fall into a profound contemplation, but the others chattered like birds. Torridon, who had in mind ten thousand tales of their taciturnity, was amazed to see them talking all at once, like enthusiastic women.

They never for an instant cast a doubt on the story of their companion, but they declared that undoubtedly he had brought a great blessing upon the entire Cheyenne people, because he had carried down from heaven an actual spirit. Upon Torridon they turned their eyes with the frankest curiosity. If he was something more than man, he was also something less than man, apparently, for they remarked frankly and openly on the slenderness of his hands and the lack of weight in his shoulders, and the delicacy of his features, which proved, they said, that he was not really a white man like those other bronzed ruffians who rode across the plains to traffic or fight with the red man.

What divine properties, then, would they expect him to have? Certainly they had seen that he ate food, cast a shadow, possessed a voice.

But they were all like Standing Bull. They never put facts

against facts. They believed what they wanted to believe, and the story of Standing Bull was too good to be thrown away. It was such an exploit as gave distinction to an entire tribe. As for the hero, Torridon puzzled over him a great deal. At last he came to the conclusion that in the first place Standing Bull had made up the story out of ecstasy and a good bit of invention mixed together, but after telling the tale a few times, had become letter perfect—and convinced himself!

He had plenty of occasions to tell the story. For the first ten days after the return of Standing Bull there was an endless succession of "feasts." Some old man would go through the camp, chanting the names of the guests who were invited to a certain tepee to "feast." The feasts were all very much like that which High Wolf had given. There was no change in the food offered, there was a great deal of smoke raised after the eating ended, and then always Standing Bull was called on for his narration.

Each time he talked a little longer. He discovered new details which were worthy of development. For instance, when he declared that his spirit had issued from his body, he said that he had looked at his lifeless self with a great deal of interest. He had leaned and fingered the back of his skull. He had admired the breadth of his shoulders and the strength of his neck, and he had looked for a while at his face, for this was the only time he could see himself except by the treacherous help of standing water or a mirror. For the first time he knew himself!

There was a great deal more of this same sort of thing added by Standing Bull, but his auditors never were tired of listening. They were not all new faces at each feast. Indeed, some of the same men attended a dozen times and always listened with the same earnest, amazed attention. Rising Hawk grew so familiar with the story that he knew when the high points were coming, and he used to rise on his knees, and even whoop with delight when he heard the never-familiar marvels of the story.

As for Torridon, the Indians treated him with a certain respect and contempt commingled. He was regarded as a part of Standing Bull, and significant simply because he was a gift from Heammawihio. He was a sort of fleshy shadow, in other words.

He was glad enough to be thus lightly regarded by these savage warriors. They were such men as he never had looked upon. There was hardly a warrior under six feet in height, and they were built like Romans, for war and effort. He saw no others quite up to the Herculean standard of Standing Bull, who was like his namesake in massive weight and power, but every man in the tribe was a powerful athlete who lived for one purpose—war! Torridon was glad to slip about among them, almost unnoticed.

Standing Bull treated him very well and made him at home in his tepee. It was a good big lodge, as befitted a man who had two wives and three children. There was a middle-aged squaw who had given her master two daughters; she was a sour-faced creature, but a strong and incessant worker. Her companion, the favored wife of Standing Bull, was called Owl Woman, though Torridon never learned why she should have been given the ugly title. She was the young and handsome mother whom Torridon had seen lifting her baby son above her head so that the child might behold the return of his father. Ill-matched as the two wives seemed to be, they got on perfectly; there was never a voice raised in the tepee except when one of the children squawled. Torridon himself was equipped with a bed, back rest, a post on which he could hang clothes and weapons.

He felt that Standing Bull might have gone on forever attending feasts and talking about his heavenly exploits, but now a cloud was hanging over this section of the great Cheyennes. Two days after the arrival of Torridon, the river which flowed past the encampment ceased running and thereafter no water was to be had except in standing pools, which shrank rapidly under the strength of the summer sun. There were plenty of other places to which they could remove to find water, but that would mean the definite abandonment of the corn crop which had been planted here. Already that corn had suffered from drought. The dusty look which Torridon had noticed had been a true sign of coming death, and if the drought persisted there might be cruel want in every lodge in the tribe during the winter to come.

In the meantime the medicine lodge was noisy every day with

the incantations of the chief doctors, making rain. But though they fasted, strained, and perspired copiously, still not a single black cloud would blow up over the horizon.

Something more than a drought was worrying Torridon. From the first he was allowed to walk about the village as he pleased, but when he asked to be allowed to mount the black stallion, Ashur, he was informed that the horse was very sick and could not be used. This, when with his own eyes he could see the big fellow galloping in the distance, the manifest king of the entire herd belonging to the tribe. When he asked for the gray mare he was given the same response, though she led home the horse herd at night by a dozen lengths when they were raced in from the pasture grounds, Ashur, like a dutiful lord of his kind, ranging in the rear and hurrying on the laggards while the Indian boys yelled like demons.

He was to be forbidden the use of a horse, then!

More than this, wherever he went, he could not make a step without close attendance. Two or three young braves were sure to spy him, and they loitered along in the vicinity, as though their own will conducted them. But after this had happened during several days, he began to understand that the Cheyennes were determined that this gift from Heammawihio should not escape from them if vigilance could prevent it.

To be sure, his captivity was not heavy, but his heart was off yonder across the sunburned fields, hurrying toward Nancy Brett and Fort Kendry. He was held here, and who could tell when the kindness of his captors might be exchanged for quite another attitude?

Nervously he waited, and as the drought increased the village grew more dusty, the faces of the Indians more solemn and sullen, just so much did the face of Nancy Brett grow clearer and dearer to him, and every day he sat with her as they had done once before, at the edge of the river where the crimson and golden forest rolled all its colors into the standing water.

On a day when he was walking past the edge of the village, with two or three braves loitering in his rear, he saw a youth of thirteen or fourteen dragging something on the ground by means of two long leather thongs over his shoulders, but when he came closer he saw that the thongs issued *out* of the shoulders. They actually were fastened to the flesh, and from either shoulder a stream of blood ran slowly down, blackening quickly with dust. Held by the rawhide thongs, a buffalo head was dragged behind the boy, who never ceased walking, though sometimes the fatigue or the misery of his constant pain made him stagger for a step or two.

"Why are you letting that boy torture himself to death?" asked Torridon of one of the braves.

"Do you think that he wants to remain a boy forever?" answered the brave curtly. "Is he to be a woman forever in the tribe? No, but a strong warrior who will go on the warpath and take scalps!"

"Can he take no scalps unless he does this?"

"If he is not braver than pain, if he is not patient and strong so that he can smile at trouble, who would want to ask him to go on the warpath?"

That answer had to content Torridon, though he had an almost irresistible impulse to cut those thongs and set the lad free. But who can free a man from self-inflicted torture?

He had hardly turned his back on that pitiful sight when he saw Standing Bull riding toward him, accompanied by no less a person than the great old chief, High Wolf. They came straight to him and High Wolf gave him a solemn greeting.

"Oh, my friend," said High Wolf, "you have been among us many days. You have heard the medicine men working to bring the rain and they raise only a dry dust. You see the corn dying by the river, and the river itself is dead. How long will it be, White Thunder, before you take pity on us and bring us the rain?"

Torridon stared in bewilderment.

"I know nothing of rain making," he said at last, with all the gravity that he could muster.

High Wolf shook his head.

"You come from the Sky People," said he, "where all these things are understood. Heammawihio will be angry with you if you let his people starve for lack of water. Come! Tell me when you will do something for us!"

Torridon looked at him helplessly, but out of that helplessness he began to evolve a thought.

Standing Bull had taken up the argument in the most direct fashion.

"If you will not do it from kindness," he said, "then we must put you in a lodge and keep you there. Let the Sky People come down and feed you and give you water. Or else, if you want anything from us, you must bring down a little rain!"

CHAPTER XXVI

★

The Thing Which Seems Good

The face of Torridon grew pale indeed at this announcement. From the moment he first came among them he had no expectation of these people, except that they would find death for him, and now that expectation was about to be fulfilled. Fire might be more terrible for a moment, but thirst would be an agony long drawn out. For three days, perhaps, he would lie in the lodge, and unless fortune send down the rain, he was a lost man!

There was perhaps one slender hope.

He said to Standing Bull: "Let you and I go a little way off and talk together."

Standing Bull went readily enough. He even dismounted, and they stood together out of earshot of High Wolf, who had wrapped himself in his robe and turned his head impatiently toward the south, for from the south alone they could expect rain at this season, it appeared.

"My friend," said Torridon to the brave, "I know that since you came back among your people and told them the great story about the Sky People and your trip to the clouds you have been looked up to as a wonderful man. But just in order to keep that reputation, are you going to see me starved to death?"

Standing Bull frowned.

"Why would it be hard for you to bring us the rain?" he said. "When I lay in the shelter that you had given me, very sick, with fire always burning inside me, death kept coming up to my side like a shadow. But you only had to wave your hand, and death ran away again. You know that I should have died many times if you had not taken care of me. When you went away to hunt I became sick and weak. When you came back I always grew strong again. You have a stronger medicine than you need to make rain."

He uttered this odd argument with perfect conviction.

"Listen to me," said Torridon desperately. "I found you by mere chance. It would have been easy for me to leave you to be washed away by the water. But I stayed with you. I took care of you. Because of that you wanted me to come to your people. I came to the Cheyennes. Now you treat me as if I am a bad man. You take away my horses. When I walk you send your warriors to watch me. And now you threaten to starve me to death unless I make rain. I cannot make rain. I know nothing about such things. In fact, no man can make rain. I speak with a straight tongue. Everything that I say is true."

He paused, breathing hard, and the warrior frowned thoughtfully upon him.

"You were not sent to me from Heammawihio?" he asked soberly.

"I was sent to you by chance." persisted Torridon. "I was wandering across the prairie. I had lost my way. I only happened to find you."

"That," said Standing Bull, "is the way that Heammawihio always works. Everything seems simple. He makes it seem so. But there is no such thing as chance. He watches everything. He sent you to me, though you did not know that you were sent."

"Suppose that he sent me to you," argued Torridon, abandoning hopelessly one part of his argument, "does that show that I can make rain?"

"Friend," said the Cheyenne gently, "I went out to do some good thing for my people and for myself. I prayed to the Sky People. They sent me you. Well, you have done something for me. You have answered that part of my prayer. Because of that I am your friend. My blood is your blood. My lodge is your lodge, and my weapons are your weapons!"

He said this with a voice not raised, but deepened and trembled with emotion.

Then he went on: "You have given back my life to me, White Thunder. You had cool hands. You killed the fire inside me. So I had one half of my prayer granted to me. Now I ask you to grant me the other half. You have done much for me. But what am I? I am only one man. All my people now are in trouble. I wish you to do good to them. Why do you shake your head? Why are you angry with me? Why do you make me sad, my brother? The great chief is very angry because you do nothing for us! Now, even if I wanted to, I could not take you away. He knows that you have great power!"

Torridon grew paler than ever, and sweat burst out on his forehead. Seeing this, the Cheyenne continued more gently than ever: "You do not need to make a great rain. Only a few drops to show that you are trying to help us. Or only bring the clouds across the face of the sky; then our own wise men can make medicine that will bring down the rain out of the clouds!"

There was no answer to make to this last appeal, and Torridon knew it. He had made an effort through persuasion and that effort had failed signally. Now he reverted to a thought which had been forming in his mind since he was first challenged.

He turned to Standing Bull as a cloud of dust enveloped them, for the wind, which had been hanging for ten days in the north, now was shifting suddenly to the south.

"Let us go back to High Wolf. I shall talk with him."

Anxiously Standing Bull led him back to the impatient old war leader, whose lips were working as he regarded the white man.

"I have talked to Standing Bull, my friend," said Torridon. "He tells me that I must really try to make the rain come. Very well, I shall do my best!"

At these words a smile, half delighted and half grim, came upon the face of the old man.

"To make that medicine," said he, "tell us what you need. We have horses and dogs to sacrifice. Also we have painted robes and many other good things, and everything that the medicine men can bring to you from their lodges you shall have—rattles, and masks, and everything that you wish."

"Brother," said Torridon, delighted with this speech, "is it true that I was sent down from the clouds?"

"It is true," said the chief, staring earnestly at Torridon's face as though he wished to make surety a little more sure.

"Well, then," went on Torridon, "if the Sky People are willing to grant my prayer, they need only to hear my voice and to see and recognize me."

"Good," said High Wolf. "I know that great things often are simply done. It is not always the largest war party that brings home the most scalps or the most horses. Can we give you nothing?"

"Nothing," said Torridon. "Only give me what I brought to your city. I had some weapons, and a pack, and two horses."

Standing Bull exclaimed suddenly.

Torridon dared not look at the warrior, who now cried: "High Wolf, this man has two horses which are as fast as the wind. Once he has them how could he be caught if he wished to run away?"

"That is true, also," remarked the chief. "And why should you need the two horses, my friend?"

"Tell me," said Torridon, his heart beating fast but his face sedulously kept calm, "in what way I was sent down from the clouds?"

"With Standing Bull. Is not that true?"

"That is true, of course. But did we come on foot?"

"No, you had two horses."

"Therefore I must have them again."

"Why, brother?"

"Because how will they know me? It is a long distance to the Sky People. They are the ones who must send the rain, are they not?"

"Yes, that is true, of course."

Delighted that his trend of thought was accepted this far, Torridon went on: "If I stand and cry from the midst of the prairie, then it is only a small sound that will come up to their ears."

"Not if the right words are used," said the chief instantly, as one sure of himself.

"I myself," said Torridon, "have sat on the clouds and heard the Cheyennes crying out for pity, and even when the whole tribe was crying out together, and the medicine men shaking their rattles, and the horses neighing, the sound came up to my ear as faint and as small as the hum of a bee, half lost in the wind."

The circumstantial nature of this account opened the eyes of the chief. He waited.

"But when I heard that small sound and looked down I could recognize the whole tribe. Now if they heard my small voice, they would look down and say, it is the voice of White Thunder. Then they would call one another and say: 'Is not that White Thunder calling to us?' And the others would come and look and say: 'It sounds like his voice, but it cannot be he. We sent him off with two horses, one white and one black, so that we could know him easily. But now he has neither of the two!'"

Broke in Standing Bull: "They would simply think that you had lost them!"

"How could I lose them?" answered Torridon, smiling. "I have done nothing but good to the Cheyennes, and the Sky People know it. They would never think that the Cheyennes could have taken my horses away from me!"

Standing Bull bit his lip. He was silenced for the moment but he was far from convinced.

Then the war chief said quietly: "What White Thunder says has a good sound to my ears. We will let him have the two horses to ride out where the Sky People may see him and Heammawihio may hear his voice."

"You will never see him again," said Standing Bull. "He will go to Fort Kendry like a bird through the air."

"No," smiled the chief. "The truth is that when we send him out we will not send him alone."

"What will you do?"

"We will send twenty braves to be around him, and all the rest of the people will be not far off to watch."

Torridon blinked. It was a mortal blow to his plan, which had been exceedingly simple—once he had the matchless power of Ashur beneath him.

"High Wolf!" he exclaimed. "What are you thinking of? To send me out, and surround me with a crowd so that Heammawihio will not be able to pick me out from the crowd?"

"I have said the thing which seems to me good," responded High Wolf. "No man can do better than his best. Now, White Thunder, go and make yourself ready to call the clouds over the sky. Standing Bull, you will bring in the two horses, the black and the silver. I shall prepare the twenty warriors to go with the rain maker!"

CHAPTER XXVII

★

A Prayer Answered

The first hope which had sprung so high in the heart of Torridon was half eclipsed by the announcement of the powerful escort in the midst of which he should have to work. But once on the back of Ashur, given half a chance to break free, he would take that chance and depend upon the dizzy speed of the great stallion to make the bullets of the Indians miss if they fired upon him.

He felt that he had a faint opportunity left, and the process of the festival might offer him a ghost of a chance.

He went back to the village with the south wind so strongly against him that he had to lean to meet it. Through staggering gusts he advanced down the street of the town.

The men were pouring out from their lodges. He felt their eyes upon him already with awe. And presently he made out one of their murmurs: "Already he has put the wind in the south! This it is to have a real medicine."

"He does not have a medicine," answered another. "He is not a mere man. He is neither white nor red!"

Torridon, facing that freshening wind, could not help remembering what he had heard over and over again during the past ten days: that the rain wind was the south wind. He looked with a sudden and frantic hope toward the horizon, but his heart fell again when he saw that all was burnished clear and clean.

He went back to the lodge of Standing Bull and there he made up his pack as it had been when he arrived. Other possessions were shifted about with perfect disregard of ownership, in many cases, but his things had been left alone with an almost superstitious regard. He took his rifle and cleaned and loaded it afresh. He saw to his two double-barreled pistols—the real pride of his life—and so he made himself ready to depart.

All this was done in the midst of a great bustling that spread through the entire camp, and finally Standing Bull called to him from without that the horses were ready.

He stepped through the flap of the tent. The silver beauty and the black were there; Comanche, the mare, looking wild-eyed from her long course of freedom in the open fields, and the stallion ten times more so. But they came like dogs to a master.

A little crowd gathered—the children pressing close, the braves remaining at a more dignified distance—but all eaten with curiosity to see the manner in which the man from the sky would handle these horses from the sky. Apparently they saw enough to stir them. Murmurs of delight and wonder rose from them. Their own animals were not trained to be pets, but to be efficient tools in time of need. Caresses were not lavished on them, and the vast majority were merely wild horses that had been caught, knowing no master except sheer force.

When he took the lead rope from the neck of the silver mare they spread out their arms to keep her from bolting away, and there were murmurs of wonder when Torridon merely turned his back on her. That murmur grew into pleasant laughter when big Ashur actually strode after his master into the tent!

So Torridon carried out all his possessions. Standing Bull bit his lip as he watched.

"Do the Sky People need to see all these things?" he asked.

"They see small and they see big," said Torridon. "Shall I have them say to one another: 'That is not White Thunder, but only a man who has stolen his horses?' "

To this, Standing Bull made no rejoinder, but his brow remained dark with suspicion. And he prominently added his finest rifle to his equipment as he stood beside the best of his own horses.

The saddling was done with much care by Torridon. He saw to it that the cinches were well secured, and that the packs were strapped on stoutly. Owl Woman helped, as in duty bound, in all this work. At last the bridles were on.

The mare was secured to the stallion's saddle by a lead rope, and then Torridon spoke. At once Ashur dropped upon one knee, almost like a human being making a curtsy, and Torridon stepped easily into the saddle, while the little boys and girls cried out in delight to one another.

Another word and Ashur rose. In his joy he rose sheer up on his hind legs, dropped lightly forward, and leaped high into the air. But Torridon knew these maneuvers. They looked wild and frantic enough to a bystander. As a matter of fact every leap and check was executed with a catlike softness and grace. It was a sort of system of play, long established between them. Not a morning passed that did not see such gamboling.

The silver mare neighed and shook her head, but followed cheerfully beside them, for she understood, also, that it was play. But the Indians looked on with alarm and wonder.

"Aha!" they cried in the hearing of Torridon. "Look! There is a man who can ride a horse. Look at that, my friend!"

"Yes, but that horse has no feet. He has wings, only we cannot see them!"

Whatever their admiration, the did not allow Torridon to proceed unescorted. High Wolf, properly enough, had given charge of the guard of honor to big Standing Bull, and that warrior took harsh command of the selected men. He had picked a score of the best mounted, most savage warriors of the tribe, and these closed in around Torridon, behind, before, and to either side, as he issued from the camp.

Behind them came a group of medicine men, hideously masked as bears, wolves, devils, fantastically draped, carrying noisy rattles. Behind these, in turn, High Wolf rode alone; and after him the rest of the tribe, following no order whatever, men, women, and children, confusedly together, rushed from the village and spread themselves out over the flat.

Well out in the open, Standing Bull led the way to a small plateau, circumscribed by a narrow and steep-sided ravine, or draw. The ground which it inclosed was almost like an island.

Here Standing Bull directed that the ceremony should take place. Torridon groaned inwardly. With the throat of this high island choked with men, the only escape would be to leap a horse across the mouth of the ravine, and that was a spring of such dimension that even Ashur well might fail in the effort.

"Now, White Thunder," said Standing Bull, "we see that you already have called the wind from the right corner of the sky. We know that you can make that wind carry thousands of clouds over us if you speak to the Sky People. Then speak to them, and tell them to have pity on the Cheyennes."

"Keep back from me," said Torridon. "All keep far back from me. Have your guns ready," he added after a moment. "Let every rifle and pistol be charged."

Standing Bull looked curiously at him. It was not the sort of request which he had expected. But he repeated the order, and the few warriors who had not already loaded their weapons immediately obeyed the suggestions.

They drew back to the verge of the little plateau. Torridon was left in the center, surrounded by potential enemies, and feeling half desperate and half foolish, like one who is a charlatan against his will.

However, something had to be done. He looked anxiously toward the south, for he had hoped that perhaps this favorable wind might bring up clouds enough to cause some slight excitement. However, there was not so much as a shadow along the southern horizon. Not a trace of vapor was floating in all the wide, hot face of the sky. Torridon sighed.

In the meantime all those hungrily expectant eyes were fixed upon him. He must do something, if only to kill time. He made the stallion kneel, and scooping up a handful of dust, he raised his hand high, and released the dust in a long, thin streamer down the wind.

The voice of a medicine man shouted in the distance: "See it and look down, O Sky People!"

Torridon raised the other arm and for a long time stared at the pale, empty vault of the heavens above him.

"Oh, Heaven," said Torridon in a trembling voice, and in

English, "if there is a heaven, help me. I don't know what to do!"

A mighty hush had dropped upon the assembly. Their eyes were riveted with tremendous concentration upon him. In the distance he could see women holding up their frightened children on high that they might have a better view. A child screamed. The cry was stifled in its midst.

Then, glancing gloomily to the south, Torridon thought he saw a thickening of the horizon line. His heart bounded into his throat. There was no doubt. The dark line grew yet broader. It began to bulge upwards in the center.

"Sky People!" cried Torridon in the Cheyenne tongue; "I command you to send the rain clouds and the rain! Instantly send them!"

At the boldness of this talk a soft groan of fear rose from the warriors and then from the masses of people beyond. Torridon shouted: "Fire! Let every gun be fired straight into the air. Standing Bull, repeat the order!"

There was no need for Standing Bull to repeat it. Instantly it was obeyed. Pistols, rifles and all, crashed their volley into the air. Wisps of smoke blew off in ragged flights. And then Torridon pointed to the south. A lofty thunderhead already was hanging in the sky.

"Swiftly, and more swiftly!" commanded Torridon. "Behold, there is the answer!"

Not until he made that gesture did a single eye glance away from him, and now all turned and beheld in the south the lofty shadow darkening the sky. There was a groan of wonder, and then followed an hysterical cry of joy.

The rain was coming! Men and women held up their hands to it. Lips parted. People began to laugh.

Torridon felt a strange lifting of the heart. He waved his hand. There was instant, utter silence, save for the murmur of children, quickly hushed.

"Not clouds only," cried Torridon, "but let there be rain, and let there be thunder and lightning."

A sort of childish ecstasy had carried him away to these words.

But now, across the rising forehead of the cloud, there was a glimmer and then a distinct streak of light.

Even the heart of Torridon was overwhelmed with awe. And from the Cheyennes there arose a cry so filled with fear that it was more like a lament than a rejoicing.

CHAPTER XXVIII

★

If They Dared

There was not so much enthusiasm in Torridon that he failed to notice that none of the braves had reloaded their weapons. Quietly he loosed the rope which bound the mare to the stallion. Follow he hoped she would, but she must not act as an impediment when he attempted to bound the black stallion across the draw.

In the meantime, the Cheyennes were beginning to give over their silence. An increasing cry of wonder and awe and joy rose from them as the cloud swept closer. It seemed apparent that it was not merely a squall. Its lofty front was crowned with great towers of the most dazzling white, based on terraces of gray, and these, in turn, were solidly founded upon a huge thickness of heavy black, impenetrable, and yet rolled fiercely upon itself.

The whole mass of vapor was in the wildest turmoil, boiling up from the bottom of the top, and sinking from the top to the bottom.

As it drew closer, it piled higher and higher into the central sky until it seemed to be occupying those spaces under the sun which the dimmest stars fill by night. Yet also it was so vast a burden that the air did not seem capable of supporting that storm, and the feet of it brushed the ground. Long arms of black were thrust down, and dun-colored mist clouded the face of the prairie.

The forward bulwark of the storm crossed the sun. At once semi-twilight took the place of what had been day, blazing hot and bright. At the same time, small streamers and flags broke away from the upper section of the cloud masses and darted like flung javelins across the heavens to the north—javelins of transparent and jewellike white which the upper sun turned into separate walls of brilliance.

Heavier arms were flung after them, darker, heavier. The whole sky to the north began to be flecked with gray and with white splashes, and then the first breath of the wind reached the watchers. It came first with a gentle sighing, and then a puff that streamed out the mane of Ashur. He, like the hero that he was, faced this towering wall of dark with pricked ears and perfect complacence. Only once did he turn his head as if to see what went on in the face of his master.

That face Torridon maintained as well as he could in a grave, almost a threatening air of command. He felt like a futile child in the presence of the deity, but he saw that it was well for him to make these grown-up children imagine that he had indeed commanded the elements.

All the time he kept an authoritative hand raised, and now again he lifted his voice in a harsh intonation, something in the tone of the chants which he had heard among the Cheyennes, though the words which he supplied were the sheerest gibberish. Covertly, he was watching the Indians of his guard.

They were overcome, like the rest of the multitude. Sometimes they glanced at him, as the raiser of the winds; but the vast majority of their attention was given to the progress of the great cloud. They drew their robes close about them. They leaned forward, as though the weight of the storm already were beating upon them.

There was only one exception, and that was big Standing Bull. Calmly reloading his rifle and a pistol which he carried in a saddle holster, he then gave his entire attention not to the wind or the clouds, but to the bringer of the rain—to poor Torridon himself! And the latter felt that he would rather have bought the indifference of that one formidable warrior than the carelessness of all the rest of the guards who were around him. He was at least glad that Standing Bull dared not leave his place at the edge of the draw.

Coward of the Clan ☆ 161

There was no doubt that the cloud was bringing copious rain with it. The mist above the face of the prairie now deepened. It became a thick wall, as impenetrable as any part of the storm, brushing the very surface of the ground, and presently Torridon could smell the acrid yet pleasant odor of rain, newly fallen upon the parched plains. The next moment his face was stung.

A cry of approbation and incredulous delight burst from the watchers as the first, rattling volley of the rain whipped them. It was as though they had taken the beginning of this to be merely a great picture, staged with vast effects of light and shadow, but perhaps as unreal as a painting on a buffalo robe. Now they saw and felt the actuality. At their feet the dust puffed up as the great drops hammered against the earth. Upon their heads and faces the volley struck. And with a universal gesture of praise and joy, they threw their arms up to the blackening sky.

The rain was indeed upon them. The overhanging coping of the cloud now was toppling down the northern sky, shutting the whole heavens away, dimming the day to evening light, and now even this light grew yet more faint. Beyond the draw were some bushes. They disappeared from sight as a gray wall swept over them.

Torridon shrank. It was like the coming of a solid wave of water. And when the weight of the rain struck him, he gasped for breath; at once, all around him was in confusion, as the half-wild horses of the guard reared and plunged, but only vaguely could he see them—figures guessed at, things out of a dream.

The very voice of the multitude was more than half lost in the roar of the rain, like the roar of a waterfall—but the chant of exultation came in vague waves toward him, split across by the neighing of the frightened horses, as the huge bulk of the cloud itself was split across by the sudden spring of the lightning. It cracked the blackened sky across from zenith to horizon, and the thunder pealed instantly afterwards. The earth shook with the sound, and the ears were made to ring.

But by that flash of the lightning, in spite of the rain curtains which streamed from the sky, Torridon was aware of Standing

Bull, who at last had left his post and was making straight for him.

He was roused as out of a trance. It seemed to Torridon, in that excited moment, that Heaven had indeed answered a prayer from his lips, and that now he was a craven and a fool if he allowed the opportunity to pass without taking advantage of it, no matter how slight it might be.

So he called to Ashur, and the stallion quivered once, and then burst into a gallop.

The silver mare, which had been crowding against the black horse as though for protection, veered far to the side, and then rushed after, whinneying. But Torridon held Ashur straight for the verge of the draw.

He had marked the place before. It was not, so far as he had been able to judge, the narrowest gap from bank to bank, but the nearer bank rounded off so as to offer a sure footing, and the farther bank was low, and rounded of edge also—such a landing place as, if a horse slipped, would not hurt him on his back, but give him a chance to scramble up, catlike.

The thunder burst on them again, with lightning roving wildly through the noise, and by that burst of light, he saw Standing Bull at the full gallop after him, guiding his horse with his knees, and his rifle raised with both hands.

"Ashur!" shouted Torridon.

And the good horse acknowledged the cry by hurling himself forward at full speed. They reached the edge of the draw. Excited voices shouted from either side, and it seemed to Torridon that hands were reached out to snare him, but now Ashur was away into the air, leaping without hesitation or fear, and flinging himself boldly over the gap.

What a gulf of sullen dark it was beneath them! And already the torrents of the rain had marked the stony bottom with little pools of water, like glimmering silver.

They shot high up, they hung in mid-air without moving forward, as it seemed to Torridon, and then they landed with a jar on the farther bank.

Sick at heart, he felt the quarters of the stallion slip away

Coward of the Clan ☆ 163

beneath him. But Ashur recovered himself like a monster cat. He scrambled, found a footing, and lurched away across the prairie, while Torridon turned back with a savage exultation in his heart.

Now let them follow if they dared!

They dared not!

On the brink behind him, he saw the great form of Standing Bull, with a rifle couched in the hollow of his shoulder.

A pressure of the knee made Ashur bound to one side like a man dodging, and that instant the rifle spat fire. The bullet went wide! Not even the sing of it came closer to Torridon's ear.

Still he looked back and saw the silver mare, brilliant and beautiful even in this rain-clouded light, hesitated on the verge of the chasm and then pitch forward into it!

CHAPTER XXIX

★

Away!

It robbed him of half the pleasure of his escape. There was nothing beneath the sun that Roger Lincoln prized more than this splendid creature, and Torridon little liked the thought of some day facing him and confessing that he had come away and left Comanche behind him.

But now he must ride hard. There was faint danger for the moment, but when the rain lifted, if it proved to be merely a passing squall, then he might well come within range of some of their accurate rifles. And with that weapon he himself was so useless that he could not well keep them at long bowls.

So he struck out a straight course to the north. He had made what inquiries he could while he was among the Cheyennes, and he had it vaguely in mind that Fort Kendry must be somewhere to the edge of the northern and eastern horizon.

"Four days and four nights," they had said, "on the warpath. Six days traveling on a hunt."

That was eloquent. He determined that he must keep steadily on by the north star for four days and nights. Certainly Ashur could do as much in that time as the sturdiest Indian ponies that ever bestrode the prairies. Having made his point, he then would venture one day to the right, and, turning back, he would go straight for two days. If still Fort Kendry was not in sight, he trusted that he would be able to circle and cut for trail until he found some path that would lead him into the frontier post. That is to say, unless what he had gathered from half a dozen sources among the Cheyennes had not been all one parcel of complicated lying.

In the meantime, he laid his course with greater and greater temporary confidence. It was true that the first blast and fury of the wind and the rain had diminished, but though it lifted, he could not see a sign of a horseman behind him. The rain developed into an ordinary pelting storm, not heavy enough to damage the corn, but certainly enough to give it the soaking it required.

Perhaps sheer gratitude in the breasts of the majority would prevent them from allowing a party in pursuit to start after him.

But he sighed and doubted that. And then his heart swelled as he remembered that Standing Bull deliberately had fired after him. Surely in all the annals of mankind there had been no deed of more foul ingratitude.

Yet, in a way, he understood. In the confused brain of Standing Bull, he appeared as a gift from heaven. The gift had no right to take wings and remove itself. Furthermore, the more valuable a gift had he proved himself—if he could cure the sick and bring the rain—the more bitterly was his loss to be regretted. No doubt, he tried to assure himself, Standing Bull had fired at Ashur, and not at Ashur's rider!

Now that he had made peace with his conception of the warrior, he felt a certain touch of kindness for the Cheyennes. Those upon whom we have lavished our kindness are always those upon whom we shower our most pleasant recollections. And Torridon felt that he had been drinking deep of real life from the instant when he first encountered the prostrate dreamer on the river island.

He told himself that he had been a boy before, but now he was a man, and a real man. Turning his head, then, from this reverie, he was aware of a streak of gray moving across the plain. He turned back with a shout of wonder and joy, and then through the rain-mist she came on bravely, tossing her head and whinneying—Comanche herself!

To Torridon, it was like the coming of a welcome and long-trusted friend. For such she was. And if he never had been able to establish in her the same sort of electric understanding which existed between him and the stallion, at least she would come when she was called, follow at his heels like a dog, and do many pretty and foolish tricks, such as sitting down and begging like a dog, with a lifted foreleg. She did a frantic circle around them, slipping in the mud as she turned, and neighing again in her rejoicing.

Then she came up beside them. Torridon could see mud on the saddle, which proved that she had rolled in the bottom of the draw. But perhaps that tumble had been the means of saving her neck. At any rate, she was unharmed, and when the rain had sluiced the mud from her, she would be as good as new.

He changed to her at once—Ashur had borne the brunt of the fast running during the escape—and pressed along the course. Into his mind, now, flashed a picture of what he had been in the first dreary days after the loss of Roger Lincoln. He had been crushed with despair, totally overwhelmed with loneliness. Now the two horses were to him like two friends, and almost filling the place of humans. Half the terror was departed from the prairies. And if he could not find his goal, he felt that he could endure hunger with calm, and trust to the luck of the hunt to find game. He was far from expert with the rifle, but still he was much improved. He had an excellent weapon, and he had an ample store of ammunition.

That first day was a hungry and miserable one, but in place of food and of warmth, he had the delicious sense of freedom. Though he scanned the horizon painfully again and again, he had no sight of any living thing, and he made up his mind that the Cheyennes, knowing how peerlessly he was mounted, had determined not to follow in chase.

He found no tree or eve a bush large enough to give shelter, when the dark day suddenly grew blacker with the evening. The best that he could do was to make a pile of the packs and then roll in a damp blanket on the lee side of the pile. A wet couch, but nevertheless his sleep was deep.

Once or twice he roused himself, always to find that the rain was pattering in his face. With vague trouble he wondered if this exposure would bring fever on him, but afterwards he slept well again, and when he wakened, it was because of the low, anxious whinney of Ashur.

He looked up. The great, black horse was standing beside him as though on guard, and Torridon sat up in the gray of the morning. The sky was still solid gray with rain clouds, but those clouds were riding high and the horizon was much enlarged since the low and misty weather of the day before. The stallion was pointing his head to the east, his ears quivering back and forth in obvious anxiety, and Torridon stared long at that spot. It was not until he had stood up that he discovered, in the gray, faint distance, faintly moving forms, barely distinguishable.

It was enough to make his heart leap. Frantically he set about saddling and bridling, his fingers stumbling with nervous haste. But he would not allow himself the dangerous privilege of another glance until he was finally in the saddle of the mare. Ashur should be reserved for the last emergency!

In that saddle, however, when he looked again to the east, he saw that danger was rapidly sweeping toward him. A dozen or more Indians, not half a mile away, were galloping toward him. They did not come in one body, but in groups of two or three, widely separated, and strung out in a line from north to south, as though they were sweeping the plains with a great net, to catch what fish they could.

He turned the head of his horse due west and sent the mare into a strong gallop. Ashur followed beside her with his enormous stride. There was no need to keep a lead rope on him. By word of mouth he could be as effectually controlled as by a bridle.

But it was only at a pace little short of her full speed that Comanche could begin to drop the wild riders behind, and that by slow degrees. The Cheyennes—he had no doubt that it was they—moved at a terrific pace, punishing their mounts remorselessly, for each warrior had three or four animals in reserve, and the horse herd was brought up in the rear by active boys, who flogged the tired ones up to the company of their fresher brothers.

Still they could not quite manage the rate of Comanche. The fine mare straightened to her work, and the Indians fell gradually off, so that Torridon felt that he could safely swing toward the north again without any danger of being caught by the wing of the enemy in that direction.

To the north he swerved, therefore, but as he turned the head of Comanche in the new direction, he heard a sound like the yelling of ten devils. And to the west, not a hundred yards away, out of the very bosom of the plain, as it were, upstarted a full score of Cheyennes, with the formidable figure of Standing Bull prominent in the front rank. They charged down at him, yelling like so many fiends, at the full speed of their horses, the heads of the ponies shaken by their fierce efforts.

Torridon turned dumb with exquisite fear.

He could call on the gray mare, but the touch of his knee and the grinding of his heel into her tender flank were enough to make her swerve and bolt back.

A bullet hummed past his head.

And, as he flattened himself along the back of the horse, he heard a voice of thunder, distinct above the rushing of the hoofs, the whistling of the wind at his ears: "Stop, White Thunder! Stop, or we will catch you with bullets! Stop, and you are safe as a brother in our hands!"

He would not stop. He had freedom, and the return to his own kind, and sweet Nancy Brett all before him. Death was not so terrible as the loss of such treasures. Desperately he rode. But he could not keep on in this direction.

Straight before him the riders from the east were storming, drawing toward him in a group, now. He could see the flogging of their arms, as they punished their horses. Their wild whoops seemed to check the pulsation of his heart.

Like what a fool had he ridden into this open trap! They simply had driven him into the lion's mouth from one side, while the other side waited to catch him. They were brushing him up, as a housewife brushes dust from the floor into a pan. He groaned with rage as well as terror.

Then he drove Comanche to the due north, or a little east of it.

She had gone well before. But her speed now startled even her rider.

He thought that he could detect a note of rage rather than triumph in the shouting behind him. Certainly the noise was growing dimmer. With unflagging speed she kept on, running straight and true.

There were two Indians on the right flank of the Cheyennes who were rushing at him from the east. Those were the two on whom the greatest share of the burden of catching him must lie, now. With a falling heart he recognized in one of them that glorious young warrior, that peerless rider and rifleman, Rising Hawk. Like a bronze statue endowed with life he came, erect in the saddle, the rifle ready beneath his arm.

His left hand was raised. He was shouting to Torridon to warn him to a halt, and the fugitive saw that he must play his last card now or lose the game forever.

He had Ashur running lightly beside him, turning his lordly head as though he scorned these men of the prairies. Now he drew the big horse closer with a single word. Shoulder by shoulder ran mare and stallion, and it was a simple thing to slip from one saddle to the next. It was a trick that he had practiced many and many a time before, and now his labor was well spent. He was on Ashur—and at his first call the big black leaped away from Comanche as though she had stumbled in full stride.

Like a human being afraid of being left behind, she whinneyed with terror, but Ashur was leaving her with every stride. They were past Rising Hawk, now. Standing Bull's party were far behind. Then Torridon heard the crashing of many rifles, yet he did not hear the whistle of a single bullet. He wondered at it. Then, glancing aside, he saw Rising Hawk deliberately fire his weapon high into the air.

At last he understood. They would frighten him into surrender if they could, but they would not deliberately harm him. And, as that amazing knowledge came to him, Ashur swept him into a shallow draw just deep enough to shelter horse and rider. They raced a furious mile along its winding course, and when they left it again to bear straight north, Standing Bull and Rising Hawk and all the rest were hopelessly behind, and every moment they were being distanced more sadly. Even Comanche, with all her speed, and without a rider to burden her, was a full two hundred yards behind!

CHAPTER XXX

★

Fort Kendry

After the foolish manner in which he had allowed himself to be so nearly snared by the Cheyennes, Torridon lost his confidence. He felt no better than a boy, and an irresponsible one, at that. But two things struck him with a lasting wonder out of this adventure. The one was the blinding speed of Ashur—for never before had he seen it so tested—the other was that the Cheyennes had chosen to spare his life.

He did not try to deceive himself on that point. He had been in their hands, to all intents and purposes. If they wanted his scalp, it could have been theirs for the asking, so to speak. The twenty rifles which had risen with Standing Bull to block his fight could have riddled him with bullets. But they wanted his life, not his death. And gravely, gravely did he wonder over this state of affairs.

In the meantime, he had the stallion and the mare to carry him, and he vowed that he would give them nothing but short halts for the next two days. Let the Cheyennes follow if they could! So he set his teeth and narrowed his eyes, and embarked upon two days of weary, continual labor and effort.

The weather broke before midday, but though the sun came out bright and clear, the going was frightfully heavy under foot. The weight of it, however, was not all a disadvantage. He was able to get fresh meat on that account, for the antelope which at last he struck down with a lucky shot was kept in range only by the softness of the ground over which it raced.

He paused to roast bits of the best of the flesh. He carried two large cuts of the antelope with him, and with them he could consider the food problem settled on that trail.

After that he voyaged through empty prairie until the fourth day out, when he struck into rolling ground, and in the distance to the north and the west there were tall mountains, dark with forests.

He came to a river, swift and mighty. When he first came to the bank, he was in time to see a drowned tree floating rapidly past and he knew that the stream was unfordable here. He would have to go higher up before it could be passed. So he turned to the left and went on for another two hours until he saw a canoe paddled in the flatter shallows of the stream by two men in frontier costume of deerskin, dark, almost, as Indians, but identified even in the distance by the sunburned paleness of their hair.

Torridon, from behind a great tree, watched them working, their paddles flashing rhythmically, and the wake dotted with small whirlpools where the wooden blades had dipped and pulled.

Rapidly they approached. The craft was long and slender, made roughly, but with infinite grace. In the center was a mound, covered with a buffalo robe. A rifle lay at the hand of either paddler, but they seemed to pay no attention to the banks of the stream until—there was a sudden shout. The steersman backed water strongly, and the paddler in the bow shipped his paddle and caught up a long rifle. Lightly he balanced it, and stared straight at the tree which sheltered Torridon.

So alert and keen did the two appear that Torridon felt as though the tree were small protection indeed.

He shouted in haste: "A friend! White man!"

And he cautiously exposed himself a little, waving a hand. The man in the bows nodded.

"Come out and show yourself," called he.

Torridon slowly stepped into view.

"What might you be aiming at?" said the steersman at this.

"Fort Kendry!" said Torridon eagerly. "Do you know where it is?"

The bowsman turned and chuckled and the steersman chuck-

Coward of the Clan ☆ 173

led as well. They let the canoe drift slowly ahead, the faint wake darkening the water behind them. There was not a sound. Then a fish leaped and splashed heavily, but still the two allowed their craft to float on, paying little heed to Torridon's question, but staring at him curiously.

"Do you know?" cried Torridon. "Is it many days away?"

He followed them along the bank, imploring: "For Heaven's sake come to the bank and tell me where I am. I've been lost—"

They laughed again. Either they were mad or else they were callous brutes!

Then, as they began to dip their paddles once more, the bowsman called over his shoulder: "Go round the next bend!"

And they swept on down the shining river. Torridon, sick at heart, looked after them until his eyes were blinded by the sun-path over the water. He had so yearned to be among his kind again, and this was a sample of their greeting!

He went back to Ashur and mounted him with a sigh. He hesitated. It might well be that the proper course was down the stream; and yet he was curious about what might lie around the next bend. He sent Ashur forward at a dogtrot, the mare following leisurely, picking at tempting tufts of grass, here and there. And so, finally, he rounded the broad bend of the stream and through the margin of trees he saw before him a dazzling flash, as though a powerful glass had been focused in his eyes. He rushed on through the trees.

It was the reflection from a window pane, and not a quarter of a mile away he saw the tall rock walls of a little fort, with three small cannon topping the walls—each gun hooded to the muzzle with tarpaulin. Around the knees of those strong bastions were scattered huts, lean-tos, dog tents, Indian lodges.

Fort Kendry!

Torridon clasped his hands together. He was very young. And his sensitive soul had been long and hardly tried. He had been through the long valley of death, as it were, and now he hardly resisted the impulse to weep, but let the hot tears tumble down his face. Sobs rose and choked him. These, out of awe of the forest silence, he kept down.

But no, that silence already was broken. Out of the distance came the brisk and ringing noise of a hammer, rapidly applied, and on the heels of it a dog began to howl—a scream of fear and pain, that died in a succession of rapid yelps.

Torridon sighed again. He almost forgot that this was the happy goal; he almost forgot that beautiful Nancy Brett was somewhere in that collection of tents and houses, or in the solid circumference of the fort itself. Between her and him there existed a thick veil of brutal humanity, and this he must try to brush aside. It seemed to poor Torridon, indeed, that the dog had cried out to say the thing which was in his own soul.

Then stifled laughter came from near by. He saw two men peering out at him, their faces convulsed with mirth. Brutal, savage faces he thought them, more brutal than the face of any Indian.

He gasped at the sight of them, and as he showed fear, a leering joy gleamed in the eyes of the larger of the pair. He thrust himself out into the trail and laid a hand on the bridle of Torridon's horse.

"What're you blubberin' about?" he asked. "Who are you, and where are you goin'?"

"And where," asked the second fellow, stepping forward in turn, but keeping a bit to the rear, "did you get them hosses? Who give 'em to you?"

"Who'd you steal 'em from, you better ask." said the first of the worthies. "Get down here on the ground and let me have a look at that hoss!"

Torridon shuddered as he heard the command. Many a time a man passed through many perils, through many dark moments, and the cup was dashed from his lips at the very moment when he had won to it.

"D'you hear?" bellowed the first speaker, and laid a hand of iron upon the knee of Torridon. "Down off that hoss, or I'll pick you outn the saddle and throw you in the river, you sneakin' thief. That's what you are! I can see it by the coward look of you. Get out of the saddle! Move!"

The miracle had happened to Torridon before, more than once, and when the supreme movement came mind and forethought vanished. A sheer physical instinct took command. So did it now. Into his hands winked a long, slender, double-barreled pistol, and he thrust the barrels straight into the throat of the other.

"Sufferin' jack rabbits—" began the big man.

He paused, mouth agape. His eyes, round and wide, read the face of Torridon as a child reads indecipherable print in a primer.

There was the other, however, to consider. He was circling catlike to the rear.

"Keep your friend back," said Torridon, "or I'll give you one barrel and try the other on him. Tell him to get here behind you, where I can keep an eye on him."

To his own amazement, the thing was done. Like two awed children they stood before him.

"Now," said Torridon, wicked pleasure coming to him, "tell me if I am a horse thief?"

The first man, rascal though he might be, had recovered from the first shock. He was able to grin down the pistol barrels.

"Son," said he, "you got the bill of sale right there in your hand. I didn't see it at first. Matter of fact, I guess you got two bills of sale."

"Then drop your rifles and back up to the trees," ordered Torridon.

It was done, in turn. They let the long guns fall—then slowly moved back, watching Torridon cautiously all the time.

"Only, will you mind tellin' me," asked one of them, "how you filled your hand? Did you have that gun up your sleeve all the while?"

He said it wistfully, and Torridon could not help smiling. Then, at a touch of his knee, Ashur moved forward. The gray mare cantered beside him. He rounded the next turn among the trees and, glancing back, saw that the pair of ruffians had not moved.

He was not overjoyed as he went on, but he had an odd interest in the knowledge that those heavy, trustworthy rifles even in practiced hands had proved but clumsy protectors at close range, where speed was of avail.

Then his heart began to lift. No doubt he was riding into a brutal society, but it might be that he would find in himself a sufficient manhood to face the members of it down.

He was entering the town. There were no streets. Between the houses the ways were simply surface soil, beaten to a deep pie by rain and the cutting of ten thousand hoofs. The horses dislodged one foot at a time, with a loud, popping sound. The pedestrians going here and there wore to a man strong boots, clotted with the mud. And altogether it seemed to Torridon the most dreary, little, patched and crazy quiltwork village that ever he had seen.

And yet it was Fort Kendry!

A thousand times he had heard that name. It had been ringing through the stories that came in from the frontier. It was one of those last outposts of civilization, hardly civilized itself. Men said that the rapid river that slid past Fort Kendry ate a man a day—and nothing done to the murderers! Still he had some doubt, and calling to a bearded, little, ratty-looking man he asked if this were indeed Fort Kendry. The latter, in reply, merely gaped, and then broke into loud laughter and went on his way.

He went further, until he saw a squaw standing with arms akimbo in the door of a miserable shack. He asked of her in English. She merely stared insolently at him, eying him with contempt, and the two splendid horses with curiosity. He tried her in Cheyenne.

She started convulsively and sprang forward. To the bare ankles she sank in the mud. Yes, this was Fort Kendry. Did he come from the Suhtai? Had he been with them long?

Yes, Roger Lincoln was at the Fort. He lived inside the fort itself. Had he known in the Cheyenne tribe a great warrior, Yellow Wolf, who—

Yes, Samuel Brett was here, and living with his niece in the big, square house just outside the gates of the fort. So she poured out answer and question intermixed. But he did not wait to satisfy her curiosity. He merely waved his hand to her and pressed forward. He was, indeed, too choked by the wild fluttering of his heart to be capable of speech.

CHAPTER XXXI

★

Nancy!

He went toward the square house which had been pointed out to him. A big man with a square-cut beard was chopping wood beside the building. His brawny arms were bared to the elbow; the ax flew like a feather in his grasp. There was something deeply familiar to Torridon in the appearance of the stalwart. And he called in a trembling voice to know if this were the house of Samuel Brett.

The other turned, ax poised for a stroke. Slowly he allowed it to sink to the ground as he stared, and then he shouted, "By grab, it's the thief!"

And dropping the ax, he snatched up a rifle. Resistance was not in the mind of Torridon. In blank terror he whirled the horse and fled, and heard the click of the rifle hammer, followed by no explosion, then the furious growling of the other.

Before him the gate of the fort was wide open—a double gate in fact, with men leaning on their tall rifles near by. Through the gate he fled, and drew rein inside, a badly frightened youth. Loud and angry voices demanded the reason for thus pushing into their midst, without leave begged. Stern faces closed around him, and a hand was laid on the bridle rein.

"Roger Lincoln!" was all he could stammer. "Is Roger Lincoln here?"

"And what d'*you* want with Roger Lincoln?" asked one when another exclaimed: "By gravy, its Comanche!"

"Comanche, you fool! She's a half a hand taller'n that gray runt!"

"I tell you, I know her. It's her! Didn't I match my pinto agin' her last year? Didn't she leave him like he was hobbled?"

A crowd of the idle and curious was gathering and suddenly, through that crowd, Torridon was aware of a tall man stepping lightly forward, his long hair gleaming over his shoulders, a jacket of the most beautiful, white deerskin setting off his fine torso.

"Roger!" shouted Torridon. "Oh, Roger Lincoln!"

Would he, too, have a rifle and curses with which to greet him? No, no! For Roger Lincoln came with a leap. He took Torridon in those slender, mighty hands of his, lifted him to the ground, and held him at arm's length, by the shoulders.

"My boy," said Roger Lincoln softly, "this is the greatest and the happiest and the finest day of my life. Lad, how did you come back to me from the dead?"

They sat in Lincoln's room in the fort. Fort, indeed, by courtesy, for it was held by a trading company and not by Federal troops. Hundreds of miles to the east the formal authority of the government ended. With an armed rabble, the fur company held this outpost; according to the whim of the moment it made its laws. Half hotel and store, and half fortress, it ruled the wild country around it.

They had interchanged stories eagerly. The tale of Roger Lincoln was simplicity itself. Out hunting, and not three miles from his starting place, he had been snatched up by a wandering band of Crows, far from their own hunting grounds. Death and scalping would have been the end of him, had it not chanced that the chief knew Lincoln to be a famous man and decided on accepting a ransom. They proceeded straight to the vicinity of Fort Kendry, and there Roger Lincoln had no difficulty in procuring a score of good horses to pay for his scalp.

That done, he secured the best mount he could find and spent two days in letting the Crows learn that no bargain could be altogether one-sided. He had pursued them, caught two stragglers, sent them to their long account, and returned, eager to get back to the spot where he had left the boy.

But of course he found that Torridon was gone. The letter placed on the site of the camp fire was gone, also. And after hunting in vain for sign which he could follow, Roger Lincoln had returned to the fort, hoping that his young friend might be able to win through to it, even against heavy odds.

Next came the tale of Torridon, hastily sketched in, to which Roger Lincoln listened with increasing joy. The trip to the Sky People filed him with laughter and excitement. And, finally, he caught the hand of Torridon and exclaimed: "You're such big medicine to that pack of wolves that they'll never give you peace. They'll be trying to steal you again, one of these days!"

"Don't say it!" murmured Torridon. "It makes me faint and weak to hear you!"

The frontiersman rested his chin on the palm of his hand and regarded the boy with the smile and a nod. "The same Paul!" he said. "The same Paul Torridon! Almost like a girl until it comes to the pinch—and then like a pair of tigers!"

"No, no!" exclaimed Torridon. "Ah, Roger, if you knew how happy I am to be with you again, and how many times I've prayed to have a man like you with me!"

Here they were interrupted by a knock at the door and no less a person than the commander of the fort appeared, a man of middle age, shrewd and hard-faced, to tell Roger Lincoln that he was accused by Samuel Brett of harboring a horse thief.

"It's the case of Ashur," said Lincoln. "Come down with me and we'll face Brett. He's not a bad kind of man. But they've written to him that the stallion was stolen, and in a way he was. Now's the time to face it out."

He would not wait to hear the protest of Torridon, who had no wish to meet that grim axman who so nearly had put an end to his days not long before. But down went Lincoln, Torridon and the post captain together, and found Brett in a high rage. He repeated his accusation in a loud voice. Torridon was a sneak and a thief and a member of a cutthroat family. And he had repaid the kindness of the Bretts by slipping away with their finest horse.

The post captain heard this speech with a growing darkness

of brow. "The law ain't overworked in these parts, much," he declared. "But a hoss thief I hate worse'n a snake—it's one reason that I hate every Indian I ever seen. And if this Torridon has stole the black stallion, back he goes to Brett; and, besides, I'll make an example of him that'll—"

"Hold on a half minute," smiled Roger Lincoln. "Let me tell you that I found Torridon locked in the Brett cellar. They intended to cut this lad's throat the next day. We had to fight our way out, and once out, we had to take the best horse on the place to be sure of getting away from the murderers. The horse that we took is the black one. We'll admit that. But I think the circumstances alter the case a good deal, don't you?"

"The sneakin', lyin'—" began Samuel Brett.

"Wait!" interrupted the commandant sharply. "Lincoln, you give me your word that you've told me the straight of it? He took the horse to escape bein' murdered?"

"I give you my sacred word."

"Then the hoss belongs to him by rights," said the other, and refusing to listen to another word, he turned upon his heel and hurried away, leaving Samuel Brett half apoplectic with fury.

Roger Lincoln had drawn Torridon to one side.

"Now, man," he said, "while I keep Sam Brett here and try to hold him, get to Brett's house. You'll find Nancy there, I think. Go fast, my boy!"

He turned to Samuel Brett.

"Brett," said he, "if you think that you have a fair claim to that black horse, will you sit down in my room and talk it over with me? Paul Torridon and I don't want to figure as horse thieves."

"I'll talk it over here!" roared Samuel Brett. "Or I'll fight it over here. As for right, I can show you—"

Torridon heard no more.

He had slipped away through the crowd and hastened through the open gates. Evening was covering Fort Kendry. Lamps were beginning to glimmer behind the windows, and the smell of frying meat made the air pungent as Torridon came again to the big square house and heard a woman's voice calling: "Nancy! Oh, Nan!"

From the distance: "Yes, Aunt Mary!"

Oh, heart of Paul Torridon, how still it stood! He hastened through the gloom toward the trees and saw a form issuing from them with arms filled with greenery. He told himself that he could tell her by the mere pace at which she walked, the lightness of her step and the sense of joy that went before her like radiance before a lamp. She came quickly on until she was aware of his shadow standing against the twilight gloom, and she stopped with a faint cry.

Then, cheerfully: "Are you the new man that Uncle Samuel sent in from Gannet?"

He did not answer. He could not!

He heard her catch a frightened breath, but instead of running from him, she came slowly forward; a small step and a halt, and a step again. The greenery slipped from her arms to the ground.

He heard a small whisper, but to him it was all the vital, human warmth of song, and then she was in his arms.

From the door a long nasal wail was calling: "Nancy! Oh, Nan, where are you?"

And Torridon whispered: "She's here! Oh, Nancy, Nancy, how beautiful you are!"

And she: "Silly dear, how can you see me?"

"I can see your goodness and your truth," said Torridon. "And I—I—"

"Nancy!" wailed the caller. "Are you comin'?"

"Never, never!" whispered Torridon.

"I have to take these in," whispered Nancy in reply. "I'll be out again in a flash. Wait here—I've got to go in—she'd never stop calling me—"

"How long will you be, Nan?"

"I don't know. Not half a minute. Not two seconds!"

"Nan, I feel as though I'll never see you again!"

"Ah, but you will."

"Kiss me once!"

"There, and there!"

She swept up her fallen load and ran into the brightness of the doorway.

Torridon heard her saying: "I stumbled on the path and quite lost my breath."

"Why, honey," said her aunt, "you look all done in. Set down and rest yourself a minute, and—"

And a hood of darkness that instant fell over the head of Torridon, was jerked tightly over his mouth by mighty hands, and strong arms caught him up, crushing him with their power!

CHAPTER XXXII

★

The Out Trail

He felt himself being carried rapidly away, and faint he heard a voice murmur, beside the robe that stifled him: "Will you be quiet and make no cry, White Thunder?"

"Yes!" gasped he in the Cheyenne tongue.

Instantly the hood was jerked from his head. They were standing under the edge of the trees, he in the huge arms of Standing Bull. He knew that ugly profile even in that faint light.

"No harm, little brother," murmured Standing Bull. "You are more safe now than you would be in your own tepee. I, Standing Bull, have spoken."

He allowed Torridon to stand, but kept a tight hold on him.

And now the shadow of the girl ran out from the lighted door of the kitchen. Torridon saw her, as the Cheyenne drew him back into the shadow of the trees, saying: "Rising Hawk has gone to bring your horse. We would not take you back on a common pony. And all shall be as you wish in the tribe. You shall be a great medicine man among us, White Thunder. You shall be rich, with horses and scalps and squaws."

The trees closed between Torridon's back-turned face and the silhouette of the girl, but faintly, far off he heard a cautious voice calling: "Paul! Paul!" And then a little louder, in a voice broken with fear and grief: "Paul Torridon! Where are you?"

A rustling passed among the trees before them. They came into a clearing and there were a dozen horses in waiting, and the gleaming, half-naked forms of several warriors. They closed in a whispering knot around Torridon. He did not hear their voices, for faintness dimmed his ears with a dull roaring through which he still seemed to hear the sad voice of a girl calling for Paul Torridon.

And suddenly he groaned: "Standing Bull, if I have been true to you, and helped you in bad times, be my friend now. Take your knife and strike it into my side, but don't carry me back to the Cheyennes!"

"Peace, peace, peace!" said Standing Bull, like a father to a sick child. "Peace, little brother. Happiness is not one bird, but many. We shall catch them for you, one by one. We shall fill your hands with happiness. Behold! Here is Rising Hawk, and the black thunder horse is with him!"

Suddenly Torridon was raised and placed in the saddle. Standing Bull stood close beside him.

"If you make a loud shout," he said, "I give you the thing for which you ask—this knife through the heart. But go with us quietly, and everything shall be well. You shall be to me a son and a brother and a father, and to all the warriors of the tribe! Rising Hawk, watch the rear. I ride in front with White Thunder. Ah, ha! This night Heammawihio has remembered us!"

And with his feet lashed beneath the saddle, and a lariat running from the neck of the black stallion to the saddle bow of Standing Bull, Torridon was carried out from the settlement. The lights gleamed more dimly through the trees and went out altogether, and presently there was the faint glimmer of water to their left.

They were well embarked on the homeward way—the out trail for Torridon, from which he could see no return.

And he raised his head to the broad and brilliant sky, where every star shone brightly, and he wondered why Fate had chosen to torment him. The sense of Roger Lincoln's faith and truth rode at his side like a ghost, and the beauty of Nancy Brett, but they had been shown to him only to be taken away.

There were no tears in the eyes of Torridon. He had found a grief too great for that.

Standing Bull put the horses to full gallop. They began to rush forward like the wind. Trees and brush and the shining river poured past them, but the calm stars hung unmoved in their silent places above him.

A special offer for people who enjoy reading the best Westerns published today. If you enjoyed this book, subscribe now and get...

TWO FREE

A $5.90 VALUE—NO OBLIGATION

If you enjoyed this book and would like to read more of the very best Westerns being published today, you'll want to subscribe to True Value's Western Home Subscription Service. If you enjoyed the book you just read and want more of the most exciting, adventurous, action packed Westerns, subscribe now.

Each month the editors of True Value will select the 6 very best Westerns from America's leading publishers for special readers like you. You'll be able to preview these new titles as soon as they are published, FREE for ten days with no obligation.

TWO FREE BOOKS

When you subscribe, we'll send you your first month's shipment of the newest and best 6 Westerns for you to preview. With your first shipment, two of these books will be yours as our introductory gift to you absolutely FREE, regardless of what you decide to do. If you like them, as much as we think you will, keep all six books but pay for just 4 at the low subscriber rate of just $2.45 each. If you decide to return them, keep 2 of the titles as our gift. No obligation.

Special Subscriber Savings

When you become a True Value subscriber you'll save money several ways. First, all regular monthly selections will be billed at the low subscriber price of just $2.45 each. That's

WESTERNS!

at least a savings of $3.00 each month below the publishers price. Second, there is never any shipping, handling or other hidden charges—Free home delivery. What's more there is no minimum number of books you must buy, you may return any selection for full credit and you can cancel your subscription at any time. A TRUE VALUE!

Mail the coupon below

To start your subscription and receive 2 FREE WESTERNS, fill out the coupon below and mail it today. We'll send your first shipment which includes 2 FREE BOOKS as soon as we receive it.

Mail To:
True Value Home Subscription Services, Inc.   12529
P.O. Box 5235
120 Brighton Road
Clifton, New Jersey 07015-5235

YES! I want to start receiving the very best Westerns being published today. Send me my first shipment of 6 Westerns for me to preview FREE for 10 days. If I decide to keep them, I'll pay for just 4 of the books at the low subscriber price of $2.45 each; a total of $9.80 (a $17.70 value). Then each month I'll receive the 6 newest and best Westerns to preview Free for 10 days. If I'm not satisfied I may return them within 10 days and owe nothing. Otherwise I'll be billed at the special low subscriber rate of $2.45 each; a total of $14.70 (at least a $17.70 value) and save $3.00 off the publishers price. There are never any shipping, handling or other hidden charges. I understand I am under no obligation to purchase any number of books and I can cancel my subscription at any time, no questions asked. In any case the 2 FREE books are mine to keep.

Name _____

Address _____ Apt. # _____

City _____ State _____ Zip _____

Telephone # _____

Signature _____

(if under 18 parent or guardian must sign)
Terms and prices subject to change.
Orders subject to acceptance by True Value Home Subscription Services, Inc.

SONS OF TEXAS

The exciting saga of America's Lone Star state!

TOM EARLY

Texas, 1816. A golden land of opportunity for anyone who dared to stake a claim in its destiny...and its dangers...

___	SONS OF TEXAS	0-425-11474-0/$3.95
___	SONS OF TEXAS#2: THE RAIDERS	0-425-11874-6/$3.95
___	SONS OF TEXAS#3: THE REBELS	0-425-12215-8/$3.95

Look for each new book in the series!

Check book(s). Fill out coupon. Send to:

BERKLEY PUBLISHING GROUP
390 Murray Hill Pkwy., Dept. B
East Rutherford, NJ 07073

NAME_____

ADDRESS_____

CITY_____

STATE_____ZIP_____

**PLEASE ALLOW 6 WEEKS FOR DELIVERY.
PRICES ARE SUBJECT TO CHANGE
WITHOUT NOTICE.**

POSTAGE AND HANDLING:
$1.00 for one book, 25¢ for each additional. Do not exceed $3.50.

BOOK TOTAL	$____
POSTAGE & HANDLING	$____
APPLICABLE SALES TAX (CA, NJ, NY, PA)	$____
TOTAL AMOUNT DUE	$____

PAYABLE IN US FUNDS.
(No cash orders accepted.)

203b